DESPITE THE ODDS 2

Taking Over

JUHNELL MORGAN

URBAN AINT DEAD PRESENTS

URBAN AINT DEAD

P.O Box 448

Maybrook, NY 12543

Cover Design: Angel Bearfield / Dynasty Cover Me

Edited By: Shawna Brim / Ladies of Lit

Contact Publisher at www.urbanaintdead.com

Email: urbanaintdead@gmail.com

Print ISBN: 979-8-9869098-6-8

SOUNDTRACKS

Scan the QR Code below to listen to the Soundtracks/Singles of some of your favorite U.A.D titles:

Don't have Spotify or Apple Music?
No Sweat!
Visit your choice streaming platform and search URBAN AINT DEAD.

Currently on lock serving a bid?
JPay, iHeartRadio, WHATEVER!
We got you covered.
Simply log into your facility's kiosk or tablet, go to music and search
URBAN AINT DEAD.

URBAN AINT DEAD PRESENTS

Like & Follow us on social media:

FB - URBAN AINT DEAD

IG: @uadpresents

Tik Tok - @uadpresents

Submission Guidelines

Submit the first three chapters of your completed manuscript to urbanaintdead@gmail.com, subject line: Your book's title. The manuscript must be in a .doc file and sent as an attachment. The document should be in Times New Roman, double-spaced, and in size 12 font. Also, provide your synopsis and full contact information. If sending multiple submissions, they must each be in a separate email. Have a story but no way to submit it electronically? You can still submit to URBAN AINT DEAD. Send in the first three chapters, written or typed, of your completed manuscript to:

URBAN AINT DEAD
P.O Box 448
Maybrook, NY 12543

DO NOT send original manuscript. Must be a duplicate.
Provide your synopsis and a cover letter containing your full contact information.
Thanks for considering URBAN AINT DEAD.

PROLOGUE

BISHOP

I laid across my king-sized bed with the light from the TV being the only light in the room. April laid next to me in nothing, but a black lace panties and bra set as she told me her plan. Honestly, it angered me, but I could never be mad at April too long for doing what she promised to always do — have my back and do whatever it took to keep our family together. I would have been able to let everything go, but this nigga couldn't let shit be. He was still gunnin' for me, and before I let a nigga get the drop on me, I would handle them first. I just didn't like the fact that April was letting a nigga think that my shit was his shit, even if it was just a part of her plan. I was ready to go in, guns blazing, and shoot that nigga right where he stood. But I guess April thought we should go about things a little differently.

I knew April wanted us to take our time when we got at Red, wanting to make sure everything went down smoothly. She felt if I just went off and killed him, shit would get sloppy and something bad would happen. So, she wanted to ensure I had a clear mind when it finally happened. We decided to make our trip to Mexico a celebration trip for me and Corn. For that time, I cleared my mind and enjoyed having all of us together. As soon as we got back home, I brought it back up. If nothing else, I didn't want him getting the first shot off or

April losing contact with him. It was time for me to make my move, and I couldn't let April talk me down anymore.

We still lived in the same house, so we weren't hard for niggas to find. I knew if anyone stepped in the home my children laid their heads in, bodies would drop, and I wanted to avoid that happening. Walking into Jasmine's room, I read her a bedtime story. April had started reading to her every night, and now, since I'd been home, it had become my job. Making sure I didn't wake her up, I snuck out the room and closed her door.

As I got closer to our room, I heard music playing. I walked in to find April laying down in bed in a light pink negligee. She'd turned the TV off and had lit several candles around the room, giving me just enough light to see. Walking over to my cherry wood dresser, I removed my du-rag and tied it around my head before undressing. Taking my seat on the edge of the bed, I took April's feet and placed them into my lap. I began massaging them softly, but all I could think about was killing that nigga, Red. I knew that April's mind was set on making love, but the only thing on mine was murder.

Pulling her feet away, she scooted down to the bottom of the bed and straddled me. I kissed her on the neck as I hugged her tightly. "Baby, you know ol' boy's time is running out, and we gotta make this shit happen."

April put her arms around my neck, leaned back, and looked in my eyes. "You want me to call him right now to set it up?"

I really did, but I said, "Or tomorrow."

"I can tell that it's fucking with your mind so let's just get it out the way." April got off my lap and walked over to her dresser. She bent over and opened a bottom drawer. As she moved some stuff around, I couldn't help but let my mind wander while looking at her thick ass. She straightened up and came back to sit next to me holding a flip phone, something that really went out of style while I was locked up.

April turned on the phone and looked at the screen. "This nigga might not even wanna talk to me no more. I got damn near a hundred missed calls from this goofy ass nigga."

I shook my head. "That's why I didn't wanna wait this long to get back with this nigga. I don't got time to be lookin' for this nigga or lookin' over my shoulder cause he tryin' to hawk me down."

"Calm down, Bishop. Let's see if he pick up before you get mad over nothing." She hit a few buttons then put it on speaker while it was ringing.

Red answered the phone. "Hello?"

It was a voice that was still fresh on my mind because I replayed everything he said on the stand almost every day since. I still couldn't believe he helped me beat them charges, especially on his own family.

"Hey, baby. Do you miss me?" April said into the phone.

It was quiet for a few seconds before he said something. "Toni?" He then said something to someone in the background before coming back. "Where the fuck you been? I've been calling you two, three times a day for the last month, and yo ass been M.I.A."

April rolled her eyes. "Yeah, baby, I know you're mad, but my mom found out that I skipped school a few times and took my phone. Then she sent me to my dad's for a month, and he didn't let me do shit."

He sounded like a bitch when he answered. "I'm saying, you could have at least called or something."

"Your number is in my phone, so I couldn't, but it's all good now. I'm trying to get with you asap."

"You miss me, shorty?"

"I'm trying to get with you, ain't I?"

"When? I can be there in an hour. Just tell me where." Red spoke into the phone. It took all of me not to say shit as I listened to this nigga talk to my girl like she was his.

"Not now, baby, but I'll call you tomorrow when I can get away. My mama still trippin'." She paused then asked, "Did they ever take that nigga to trial?"

"Yeah. I said exactly what you told me to say, and he got out, so now I need you to help me get him like you said you would."

"Don't even worry about that. We can talk about it when we meet up, okay?"

"That's cool, Toni, but we need to make it happen. He gotta go," Red spoke.

They said a few more words that I didn't give a fuck about. I wanted to laugh at how stupid he was to fall for this shit, but I thought of Lil Tone and how this would be the second nigga I saw let some pussy lead him to his own death.

When April hung up, she threw the phone to a chair across the room and climbed back on my lap. "Penny for your thoughts?"

"It ain't shit. Just taking note on the power of pussy and how I hope I'll never be stupid enough to be led blind by it."

"Baby, the pussy doesn't have the power. The niggas have a weakness."

"Yeah, I guess, but all the same, I don't want that weakness to be my downfall."

After several moments of not saying anything, April asked, "So, do you want me to do this?"

I hadn't given that part much thought and said as much. "I really don't know, but I want his bitch ass to suffer. What do you think?"

She thought about it for a minute before she answered. "While you were locked up, Bull had his dogs on the block. One day, some stupid crackhead started acting crazy. Bull said one word, pointed at him, and they surrounded him, looking like they were going to eat his ass. That made him calm all the way down, but I wanted to see them dogs do their thing."

I gave it some thought but didn't like it and came up with another plan. "I don't want to put nobody else in our personal business, but I think we should burn his bitch ass."

April pushed me back flat on the bed. "I got a fire between my legs, so can we please forget about that til tomorrow and handle this business? You got a lot of making up to do."

Needing to hear no more, I grabbed her and switched positions, putting me on top of her in the middle of the bed. "This what you want, shorty?"

"Yes, please."

I wasted no time getting her naked. I leaned down between her spread legs and kissed her pussy slowly, ready to taste every drop of her honey sweet juices. April let out a moan. "No, Bishop, save that lovemaking shit for another time. I'm trying to get the dick. Fuck this pussy like you mad at it."

I only had boxer briefs on, and I didn't bother to pull them all the way down as I put my dick between her legs, entered her, and fell in balls deep. For the next hour, my thoughts were on reclaiming and making sure April knew that her pussy belonged to me.

WE STUCK TO OUR PLAN, waiting until it got dark before April called Red and told him to meet her at Ogden Park by the field house, which wasn't far from where he lived on the south side. April said that she knew the area good enough since that was where they kicked it whenever they hung out. She felt that it was the best place where we could get in and out with the least amount of risk, so I had to trust her judgment.

Other than living in Addison and going to Mexico, I'd always been on the west side of Chicago. The night that I got shot was my first time going to the south side, and I paid attention to everything. So, it was like déjà vu as April pulled off the Dan Ryan expressway on 63rd Street.

The train station lit up one side and was still busy even though it was almost midnight. Looking ahead, I saw the hospital that they took me to after I got shot. When April turned, we passed a school, and when we got to the neighborhood, it was like a ghost town. On the west side, it would've been at least a few niggas out hustling every few blocks. We took most of the same streets as I did with Bull the last time, I came out here for these same niggas. Everybody in his stick-up crew was killed that night except him. And since he had every intention on taking the stand against me to get me life in prison, I had to finish what should've been done that night. Kill everybody that had something to do with that night.

A few blocks away from the park, April pulled over and told me to get in the trunk. Getting out the car, a light drizzle had just started. I checked my banga as she opened the trunk. With one up top, I climbed in the spacious Cadillac trunk, a car that I planned to get rid of like everything else after this so that I could start fresh.

It seemed like it took a long ass time to get there, but finally, I felt the car slow down and come to a stop. I heard the door close and wondered if she got out or if he got in until I heard her voice close to the trunk.

"I got a surprise for you in the trunk. Come check it out."

I gripped my pistol a little tighter when I heard the trunk pop.

When he pulled it open, I saw his face light up like a kid on Christmas morning, but when I raised the gun and pointed it at his face, he surprised me.

"Man, fam, I know what our beef is, but shorty ain't got shit to do with this. Just let her slide and I promise she won't say shit. Let him know, Toni."

While he was pleading for April, I got out the trunk with my banga still pointed at him and went to April's side, laughing at him. We were in a dark corner of the parking lot. Even with everything around us, we couldn't be seen. April had picked a good spot that was ducked off behind several trees. He started to say something, but I stopped him. "Shut yo bitch ass up." I put my arm around April. "See, while you was on some police shit, my baby had her own little plan for you. Ain't that right, *April*?"

April stood on her toes and kissed me on the neck. "I told you, baby. I'll have your back, no matter what, and tricking this lame wasn't even a piece of what I'll do to keep our family together."

I didn't know if the look on his face was more hurt or anger after April spoke. "But..." was all he could say.

"Well, we ain't got all night. Get his keys, April. Let's put him in the trunk of his car." He was parked right next to us, and as she took the keys out of his pocket and went to open his trunk, I put the banga to his chest.

"What, you gonna kill me now? I'm the only reason you're not in prison right now. Or did you forget about that shit?" Red spoke, finally finding his voice.

I laughed. "Thank you for that. I don't know if I'm going to kill you or not, but I know that yo ass is about to get in that trunk."

"What you want, some money? I got about ten thousand put up, but that's chump change compared to the shit you're doing out west, so what the fuck you want?"

"For you to get the fuck in the trunk and shut up." He started to climb in, and I couldn't resist the urge to slap him with the banga. He let out a scream and started yelling but stopped when I didn't hit him again.

When he was in the trunk, I put my banga in my waistband and grabbed the gas can from our trunk. His eyes widened when the first splash of gasoline hit him. He quickly realized what was happening and began pleading for his life.

"Come on, fam! Fam, don't do this shit! I swear that shit over with! I promise on my dead people I'll forget about that shit if you just let me go home!"

Having heard enough of his begging, I attempted to close the trunk, but Red refused to go out easy, trying to fight his way out of the trunk. I pulled my banga back out and pointed it at him. "One way or the other, I'm going to get this closed. It's on you how I got to do it."

"You still got a chance to live, but if you say another word or keep fighting, he'll have to kill you for sure," April announced, looking down at Red. He stopped fighting and looked at April, allowing me to close the trunk.

That's one stupid nigga. I shook my head and poured the rest of the gas over the car until the can was empty.

I was just about to light his ass up when April stopped me, letting me know she wanted to move her car before I started the fire. I was so ready to kill this nigga that I almost blew up our ride home in the process.

"See, if you would've kept shit in the streets, I would've been able to let that shit go, but my girl had to go through a bunch of extra shit just to get you to do what you should've done from the start. So, rot in piss with the rest of them bitch niggas," I spoke through clenched teeth.

He began kicking and punching the trunk, screaming for help. I thought it would've been hard for me to go through with killing someone like this. It wasn't shit for me to pull out my banga and blow a nigga's brains out his head, but burnin' a nigga alive was something different. However, as I stood there, ready to set this nigga on fire and listening to Red's screams, I began to laugh.

Seeing that April was out of the way, I didn't think twice about lighting the gas can. With the can on fire, I threw it in the backseat and watched as the flames began to grow. I stood there, mesmerized, looking at the flames turn from orange to a deep yellow. Red's screams were like music to my ears as he tried to fight his way out the trunk to no avail. Standing there, watching myself burn another man alive, let me know just how much of a savage I'd become. While fighting for my life in a cell, I came to the conclusion that I could be a victim of my past or a product of it. I wasn't about to feel sorry for choosing the latter.

I walked away from the burning car and got into the driver's seat of my car before pulling off, watching the flames grow bigger in the side mirror. I drove back home, happy that my last piece of street business was handled.

CHAPTER ONE

Bishop

CLOSING THE DOOR TO MY ONE-YEAR-OLD SON'S BEDROOM, I WAS happy he was finally sleeping. He had been running around all day, getting into everything his little hands could touch. Raising these kids was damn near harder than running a full-scale drug operation, and my ass was tired.

I knew that April was waiting for me in bed, but I needed some fresh air. I bypassed the hall that led to the master suite of our mid-century, crushed stone, mini mansion. The house was beautiful and more than I ever dreamed of living in. The five-bedroom, four-bathroom home was truly the fruits of our labor, and I couldn't be happier. Giving my children the life I didn't have was every parent's dream, and I was living it.

I walked down the curved staircase which was lit by a beautiful crystal chandelier. I caught myself smiling, something that April and Jasmine said I did every time I walked past the front room. I called it the white room because of its color theme. Mama Kelly helped us decorate the house, and the most money went in this room. Every piece of the furniture was pearl white, a couch and two single chairs. There was a small table on both ends of the couch and center table made out of crystal, which was the only piece of furniture in the room that wasn't all white. The room looked like something out of the magazine, and I'd worked for it all.

I opened the front door and stepped out into the warm night air. I looked down at our S shaped driveway and saw that April had left her favorite Lexus out. She had two, but she loved the white one.

We lived five minutes outside of Chicago in Oak Park. Our house had a huge black fence around it, making it safe to leave the cars out. Our lives had been different since we left the game, so everything seemed safe to me.

Some people talked about how life was boring after being in "the game", but the smart hustlers knew the hustle never stopped. Most people that got a chance to leave did so with more money than they could spend in a lifetime. They used that money to make more money, so they could travel, party, and do whatever else they wanted. I didn't understand it at first, but since I'd been out the game for a while, I could see where they were coming from; the power was gone, the plotting and planning of our next move was over. All that shit was done, but I looked at my life and the lives of all the people I considered to be my family, and it was nothing I could complain about.

When we were doing our thing in the streets, we were stacking money, and it was coming in faster than we could spend it. We knew that we'd be straight once we completed our agreement with José and Jesus, and they hit us with an *appreciation pay* as they put it.

Really everybody did good with their money but Bull, who didn't want to leave the streets right then. He took all his guys up to Milwaukee, and it didn't take nothing for them to take over the streets up there. Only thing was, he wasn't a drug dealer, and after a year, he got tired of it. At first, he was going to join the Army, saying it was the only legal thing that sounded fun. But he ended up running into an ex-Navy Seal trying to start his own security firm and was willing to train anybody. Bull took it a step further and put most of the money up. So, he owned some of the business and brought in most of his guys who didn't have a criminal record. He was still training, but they were ready to open their office in Chicago any day now.

The twins surprised the world when they stopped smoking weed. Both went to school and now had regular jobs. In all the time we'd known them, we found out their real names when we went to their graduations. Kayla became an accountant, and Jayla worked at a law firm as a legal assistant.

While I was in jail, April and Lucky somehow found the time to start taking classes to become nurses. Once they finished, they started working at a doctor's office but had to take a lot of time off since me and Blacky started getting them pregnant back-to-back. I was trying to start my own football team. So, I was going to put as many babies inside April as she would allow.

April gave me another baby girl, who we named Rose, and a boy who we named John Bishop Thompson Jr. We said we were going to wait a few years before we had another one. Lucky had two more boys and said that she wouldn't stop till she had a girl.

Since Mama Kelly was always the one to watch the kids, it seemed only natural when she and Amanda bought and opened a daycare center. It was doing good due to a government contract Amanda secured.

Me, Corn, and Blacky didn't know what to do at first. We were running around like chickens with our heads cut off until Mama Kelly asked us to help fix up one of her apartment buildings. Subsequently, we decided to go to trade school to learn everything we needed to buy and resell houses and apartment buildings. Blacky even went and got his dealership license. So, we invested in cars as well and were making good money on both endeavors.

Now, would you call that a bad life? I didn't think so, especially when you thought about where I came from, how it all started, and the shit we had to go through to get here. Naw, it wasn't bad at all. We lived a life and created wealth for our children, so they wouldn't have to go through what we did. That was the goal, and we accomplished that times ten.

"Bishop, what the hell you doing outside?" April's voice pulled me out of my thoughts from the Ring camera behind me.

I turned toward it, knowing that she could see me, letting her know I just needed some air and would be back inside momentarily. I just needed a moment to myself to gather my thoughts.

"If you don't get up here right now. Got me waiting and thinking you was putting the kids to bed."

I laughed, knowing this was something I did every night after putting the kids to bed. This was my alone time, a time for me to breathe in the fresh air and collect my thoughts. Sometimes, I had a drink. Other times, I had a blunt. Either way, I was chillin', and now, I'd just been caught.

"You know that you didn't put yo car in…"

"Get yo ass up here right now, Bishop. Now!" April yelled, not allowing me to finish my sentence.

I walked back in the house and after closing the door, set the alarm. I took the stairs two at a time. I looked into all the kids' rooms one last time to be sure they were still sleep before I headed to our room.

Our master suite was my second favorite room in the house. The color theme was royal blue and silver, and April did her thing with the decor. An Alaskan king-sized bed set in the middle of the room with sliver silk sheets and a royal blue velvet comforter. I'd let April put what seemed to be a hundred pillows all over the bed. I couldn't lie. The shit looked nice, but they were a bitch to get off when a nigga was drunk. She had over twenty thousand dollars work of art in our room alone, along with several other silver and blue decorations.

April was lying across our bed on her stomach. I walked over to her and smacked her ass before watching it jiggle. I licked my lips as my dick stiffened a bit, knowing I was about to get some of that gushy from my woman. April rolled over onto her back and put her legs straight up in the air, giving me a front row seat to her freshly waxed pussy.

"I been waiting on you for too long," she spoke, licking her lips.

Without saying another word, I began to undress. I knew we agreed to wait a few more years before having another baby, but the way I was feeling, I might put another one in her ass tonight. Her ass had gotten fatter since she had the kids, giving April the body most bitches would pay for. Getting on my knees in front of her, I pulled her down closer to me and positioned my head between her legs. I licked slowly as her soft moans began to fill the room. I kissed her love button, savoring every bit of her. I'd just gotten into my rhythm when the landline began ringing.

"Shit!" I grabbed the phone before it could ring a second time and hoped like hell it didn't wake up any of the kids, especially Junior. When he got woken up, it took forever to get him back to sleep.

"What!?" I didn't care who it was. I was ready to cuss whoever it was out.

"Turn it to channel seven. Hurry up!" Corn said out of breath.

I motioned for April to turn on the TV, but when she did, there wasn't shit on, just a bunch of commercials. I didn't have time for this bullshit. Not only had this nigga just interrupted me getting it in with my baby, but he called me on the damn landline, which was only supposed to be for emergencies.

"Give it a minute."

I was still heated and didn't try to hide it. "Why the fuck ain't you call my cell phone?"

"Because you wouldn't have answered it as fast or at all."

I laughed. He had a point. Otherwise, I would've cussed him out. "Yeah, but if you wake up any of April's kids, you're coming to get them."

"I'll just pass them off to Moms. Tell April I said what's up," Corn spoke.

Breaking news flashed across the screen.

"Here it goes now," Corn informed.

"I'm watching."

A lady came on the screen, and I could tell she was in the hood. The first thing I thought was that somebody got killed. I got a funny feeling because the only reason Corn would call for this was if it was somebody I knew. Just as fast as the thought crossed my mind, it left when the lady started talking.

"Hello, I'm reporting live from the west side of Chicago where there has been a joint task force involving Chicago PD, FBI, DEA, ATF, ICE, and other surrounding area police departments, including Illinois State Police. They started what they're calling Operation Reputation. They said in a statement this operation would put a hold on drug sales in not only Chicago and Illinois but the entire Midwest. The police have not yet released any names, but they said for the last five years, they have been working to gather information leading to major players in drugs and gun sales. This morning, starting around 4:30 a.m., two blocks from where I stand is where they say the top dealer has been living and where they captured him as he slept. They also took down other key players all over Chicago. In the statement by the police, they seized over fifty million dollars in drug money. They believe they also got what could have been the shipment that was meant to supply the entire Midwest and is valued at street level to be worth close to a half billion dollars, the biggest bust in history on a street level operation. This is your ABC 7 eyewitness news; we will continue to bring you live updates as we receive more information on this story."

CHAPTER TWO

Bishop

One Month Later...

Since the bust, the streets had been a war zone. The police had been locking niggas up by the boatload, but some knew what it was and held court in the streets. It was a bloodbath all over the city with cops and hood niggas dropping like flies. The streets were more dangerous than they had ever been, and with niggas hungry, they were willing to do whatever they needed to do in order to eat.

What we had going on with our little house business was cool and all, but I was getting bored with the life outside of the drug game. Seeing what was going on and realizing we only missed the whole investigation by a year, I was more than happy that we were out. I mean, who in their right mind would even consider going back to that life after seeing what went down, especially when money wasn't ever going to be a problem again?

The one person I hadn't mentioned yet was Hectic. He was part of something bigger than my little team. He moved up in the ranks that had him on the move most of the time, but no matter how busy either of us got, we still spoke often, getting together at least once a month and catching up. As much as he wanted me to put my team back together, I knew keeping my hands clean for my family was more important.

He was the first person I thought about after seeing the news because he came to Chicago every time a shipment came in. We were going to get together that week, so I was hoping he didn't get caught up too.

A few days later, he called, and I was relieved to find out he was good. However, when his calls became more frequent, I knew he wanted more. So, it was no surprise when he told me he was coming to the city three months after everything went down and wanted to know if I could meet up with him; his request didn't sound to be a social meeting.

The day of my meeting with Hectic came rather quickly. Although I knew exactly what he wanted, I wasn't too sure if I could even go back to the game. The life April and I had made for our family was the most important thing, and I couldn't allow anything to take me away from that. I also wasn't sure how April would react to the meeting. I'd yet to tell her, but once I was finally dressed and ready to walk out the door, I let her know where I was going. She didn't even seem surprised. It was almost as if she already knew what was up. I knew the police still had the block hot, so I made sure to move cautiously. Not even wanting to drive my car to Hectic's location, I parked my car and took a taxi to the Hilton hotel.

I got out in front of the tall downtown building, and thankfully, there was an overhead covering since it was pouring down raining. The crisp air hit me, and I wished I'd taken the time to grab a jacket. An older, Black doorman opened the door as I walked up and nodded his head at me as I walked through the door. Looking around the lobby for Hectic, I spotted a group of businessmen dressed in suits and holding briefcases. There was a mom and dad with their two younger kids standing at the front desk. However, as I looked around, I still didn't see Hectic. He hadn't given me a room number or anything because he'd told me he would be in the lobby when I arrived. Looking over to the other side of the lobby, I saw an entrance to the hotel bar and began walking toward it. That was until I saw Hectic standing over by the elevator. He was dressed in a suit just like the businessmen that stood around him.

Walking over to him, I stood next to him as he pressed the button for the elevator. He didn't so much as speak to me, which caught me off guard. I shrugged it off, thinking he didn't want to speak in front of everyone inside the crowded lobby. However, when we got onto the elevator and he still didn't speak, I wasn't sure what was up. I followed him until he stopped at a room and fumbled with the key card. It wasn't until we were inside the room that he finally spoke to me.

"You haven't been seeing anybody watching you, have you?" Hectic asked, being sure to put the deadbolt on the door.

"Truthfully, besides today, I haven't really been paying any extra attention, so I wouldn't have noticed if they were."

"Did you change up what you do every day since they started all of this?" Hectic continued grilling me.

"Shit, I really didn't see no reason to. They said the investigation started a year after I got out, and everybody that I was close to is still out, so there's nobody that can put me in it. I don't see them coming for me. What about you?"

He turned and walked off, making his way to the mini fridge in the kitchen area of the suite. He grabbed two flute glasses off the counter and poured up. "You want a drink?"

I declined.

"Suit yourself." He shrugged, placed one of the flute glasses back on the counter, and walked back to me. "Come. Sit with me."

He took a seat at the dining room table, and I sat right along with him. Although I did drink socially, Hectic was making me entirely too nervous, and I needed to have a clear head in case anything went down.

"Man, this has been the longest three months of my life. If they would've waited another hour before taking down that shipment, they would've had me."

He looked calm about it, but the thought of losing Hectic in that moment fucked my head up. I shook my head. "Damn, that's crazy. But that means that you're in the clear now, right?"

"Yeah, I'm good now. It's the only reason we're talking about this," Hectic answered.

"I trust your word, but how can you be so sure?"

"Because I purposely caught a DUI. If they wanted me, the Feds would've got me right then." He laughed.

"That was a stupid ass risk. Why would you do that?" I asked in confusion. There was no way I would have risked my freedom like that, and I couldn't believe Hectic was moving so sloppy.

"Because my bosses don't want them people to reroute on me, and they end up losing more of their business partners. While it was a risk, it was a move that I was willing to take because I know the next move, and I want to be part of it." Hectic took a sip from his glass. "You know how the brothers are, so it should come as no surprise that they've had people following you for the last month. They don't think you have anything to worry about. Yesterday, they gave me the green light to go ahead and start putting things back in motion. They told me to sit down with you and see if you would be willing to talk with them."

"What they wanna talk about?" I asked, perplexed, not under-standing what was going on. I didn't know the nigga Hectic worked for, and if I did get back in the game, I wasn't sure about being in busi-ness with them.

"Come on, hustler. You know what they want to talk about. It's not them… yet… It's me asking you would you be willing to have another run at it?"

"You know I got to talk to April first. I don't know how she would feel about that, but if she agrees, when do you need an answer by?"

"It's no rush, but to be straight up with you, they're willing to do almost anything for you to say yes. So, if it's anything that could sway y'all, just say it, and it could probably be done —_of course within reason. Point is, they kind of need you more than you need them right now."

"How the fuck is that even possible? I been out the game for years." I didn't understand why they needed me so badly. These niggas had been in the game while my ass had turned into a family man.

"They're missing a person that's loyal, honest, and reliable. That's why they will go the extra mile to have you. Those are things that can't be brought, and they don't have the time to teach it. They know what they're getting with you. Your name rings bells in these streets, nigga."

"Is it even safe to get back out there right now? I ain't got no time to get caught up again," I spoke, looking into his eyes, so he knew I was serious.

"No, but you know we won't do nothing until all of this shit is over," he assured.

I nodded solemnly, in deep thought. "Bet. I'm gon' need a few days, but I'll get back at you."

Leaving the hotel, I couldn't help but started thinking about what I was going to say to April.

APRIL

As soon as Bishop left, I really thought of following him. That was one thing about him. When it came to me, he couldn't hide shit. I knew there was more to the meeting than them playing chess.

I decided to put my own plan into play by calling Corn and Blacky over to the house. The way I saw it, Hectic had a plan, and Bishop might not be with it. But if I could get Corn and Blacky to get on board then Bishop would fold. I needed to see where everyone's head was because if there was a chance to get back in the game then I was going to. I had some unfinished business to complete, and that shit needed to be handled.

It took them a few hours to finally show up. The family all had access to the front gate. So, when I got the alert on my phone, I ran downstairs and met them at the front door. Still in their work clothes, they stood there, and I didn't give them time to say anything. I almost yelled what I had to say.

"Bishop left this morning to have a meeting with Hectic."

Blacky looked to Corn then back at me and shrugged. "He do that every month. So, what?"

"Before we try to put this together, can you invite us inside and not leave us standing in the rain please?" Corn asked.

"My bad, bro. My ass got too excited. Come on in and close the door behind you." I walked down the hall, leading them to the back of the house. "Y'all sit down while I get y'all something to drink."

I walked into the kitchen, which was my favorite room of the house. All the appliances were stainless steel with white granite countertops. The light gray subway tile backsplash was my favorite part. Bishop tried to talk me out of it when I picked it out, saying he didn't like the pattern, but once it was on the wall, he loved it just as much as I did. I kept the refrigerator stocked with all kinds of pops for the men and water for myself. I grabbed a drink for all of us and turned around to see them sitting at the kitchen table.

Blacky was the one that didn't waste any time getting back to it. "Like I said, he do that every month."

"Yeah, I know, but I just got a feeling that something is different this time."

"I'll never argue with a woman's intuition." Blacky sighed and sat back. "So, what's different this time, April?"

"He's tryna get back in the game," Corn answered.

"Or Hectic made the offer and Bishop is going to go or already said no." I let that set in, but when no one said anything for a full minute, I asked, "So, what y'all think?"

"It really don't matter. If he don't want to do it, we shot. Hectic is his connect, and without him, we don't got shit," Corn replied.

"Plus, I wouldn't want to do nothing unless it was all of us," Blacky spoke.

"So, would y'all be down for another go at it if he accepts an offer from Hectic?" I asked, finally asking the question I brought them here for.

Together, they said yeah, and right then, I knew we were back. I couldn't hide my excitement, but Blacky fucked that up.

"But what if he said no?" he asked.

"Then we change his mind," I said with more confidence than I really had. The truth was, I didn't know if Bishop would be down for this at all. For these last five years, our lives had been strictly about our family. I just hoped if he saw we were all down, Bishop would be too.

"Yeah, that sounds easier said than done, but if you really think it's possible then I'm rocking with you," Corn announced.

I thought that it could be done. So, I left it at that, and we waited for Bishop to come home. We sat there, lost in our own thoughts, before we started talking about everything other than what was really on our minds.

Finally, we heard Bishop come in. When he walked in the kitchen and saw us all sitting there, he paused. The look on his face was like a kid that just got caught doing something wrong. I knew then for sure that I had been on point about Hectic making him an offer.

"So, what y'all on?" he asked, taking his seat next to me.

"That's what we wanna ask you, homie," Corn said, staring at him.

"How the hell did you know?" he asked, looking over at me.

"Answer what he asked you, Bishop," I spoke, nodding over at Corn.

"Well, since it's so obvious, I don't have to tell y'all that they want us back, and let Hectic tell it, they're willing to do damn near anything to make it happen."

"So, what you say?" Corn asked.

"I told him that I'll have to holla at April first."

Blacky held his hands up. "Oh, so you didn't need to holla at me or Corn, just April?"

"Yeah, first. Don't look at me like that. You don't have to live with her," Bishop spoke, only half joking.

"Damn, right. My baby ain't stupid," I said, fucking with Blacky.

"And even if she would've said no, I was going to get y'all to help change her mind. I already knew y'all would be down if the situation was right," he continued.

"So, you back in?" I asked, knowing we all wanted to know the answer.

"Even if I wasn't, I think y'all already made the decision. If y'all with it then without a question, I'm ready to do this shit again." Bishop smiled as he looked over at me.

I couldn't control myself and jumped on his lap, kissing him. "Finally, I have something real to do. I thought that I was going to die from boredom."

"Damn, y'all felt that way too?" Bishop asked, looking over at Corn and Blacky. When they both said yeah, he continued. "Y'all should've been said something. I could've had us back in a long time ago."

"Any time before now then we would've been in jail with everybody else." Corn stood from the table. "Fuck the could haves and all that. What are we doing now, Bishop?"

"How about everybody go do them, and we get back up tomorrow?" Bishop suggested.

We got up, and as we walked off, a thought popped in my head. *I am about to be the next queen of Chicago.*

CHAPTER THREE

Bishop

I SAT ON THE GRAY SECTIONAL IN THE FAMILY ROOM AS I AWAITED Corn and Blacky's arrival. I'd been in deep thought since yesterday, and I wasn't entirely sure I wanted to get back into the drug game. It was too hot in the streets right now, and the last thing I needed was to be away from April or my kids. However, if we could come up with an airtight operation and ensure everyone's freedom, then I didn't see why we couldn't get back to the hustle.

Even though Corn wasn't involved in our business before, I knew that he could run shit just like me and April could. Blacky was a big part of our operation, especially when it was just him and April. So, I was confident that if needed, any of us could lead the team.

April was behind me in the kitchen, getting drinks and snacks ready. You would think Corn and Blacky weren't eating at home because they were always hungry every time they walked through our door. April walked over and handed me a Corona.

"They're here, baby. I'll go let them in," April informed, walking away to open the door. She let them know they could help themselves to the sandwiches and drinks in the kitchen, knowing they both would.

They both thanked her before walking into the family room, plates in hand. The sixty-five-inch TV was on, but no one watched it. Everyone's mind was on something else, and we all knew what that was.

"What's good, homie? You look like you're thinkin' real hard," Corn spoke, taking a bite of his sandwich.

I leaned my head back and took a deep breath to calm my thoughts before looking at Corn. "Yeah, I want this to go right. It ain't shit that we can't figure out though."

"Okay, what's on your mind? We can talk it out cause I want to have a plan in place, so we can stick to it and not get jammed up like them other niggas did," Corn spoke.

April came and sat down on my lap with a cup in her hand. I took a sip from my beer before speaking again. "The way I see it, if we're all with making this move, then we're in it together. It's four of us, and if we put up the same amount of money, then we split the profit and duties equally amongst each other."

Corn was the first one to speak up. "Yeah, homie, only if it was that simple. It worked for what you were doing last time. But if we wanna make more money this time, we're going to need a solid plan. And everybody needs to know their parts and stick with it."

Even though it seemed they were all looking at me for answers, the fact was all of them had more time in the game and knew more about the streets than I did.

"Okay. What do you think we should do then?" I asked, turning to Corn.

"Bishop, everybody here is family, right?" Corn asked.

"That's a stupid ass question. Y'all know this is the only family I ever had besides my mama."

"And I'm sure everybody else feels the same way." Corn looked to Black and April, who both nodded. "And I don't want that to be fucked up over nothing, especially money."

"That would never happen. I'd rather be broke than not have y'all." I was confused by where this was going, but I let him continue.

"I believe you, homie, but I've seen crazy shit happen over money. So, to be able to have our family and money too, we need to be on the same page. And while I'm not trying to be greedy, especially with all the money we're going to have coming in, how fair do you think it'll be if you and April bring in fifty percent of the money?"

I thought about it and was about to answer when April jumped in. "So, you saying cut me out and split everything three ways?"

"Come on, April. It's not cutting you out of nothing, but it's like you and Bishop is a package deal, just like Blacky and Lucky and me and my moms. Everybody will do their parts, but it's going to be split between our three houses."

"Oh, I understand on the money side of things. If we put up the numbers like we were before, then a third won't be peanuts, so we're all good on that level," April said. "The one thing I'm not moving to the side on is the decision-making. Not to throw it in you boys' faces, but don't forget I pretty much ran the whole operation while the two of you was locked up."

"Damn, baby, put the guns up. We all know you're the boss." Everyone laughed except for her.

"You're going to pay for that, boy, but I'm not playing. When choices need to be made, we all have a say so."

"What's your thoughts on all of this?" Corn asked, looking over at Blacky.

"Real talk, all this shit is new to me. I'm used to selling packs or, at the most, running the joint. Besides the stuff y'all had me doing, I don't know nothing about being in a higher position."

"Okay, what about you, Bishop? You got something else to say?"

I shook my head, and Corn said, "Okay, cool. First to what you said, April, we would never try to kick you off the table. We need you as much as we need each other. I was in the game for all of them years and made some good money, but y'all counted your first million before and without me."

I cut him off. "That's not true. You helped us get in the game, and we put up over a mil for you."

"Well, besides that, y'all put the work in. And as April said, she ran it without us, but this ain't a joke. In a way, she is the boss. Now that won't mean you run things, but you proved your worth, and we all know that we can depend on you." Corn turned to Blacky. "Blacky, my nigga, I remember when you first started to hustle, and if the drug game was like corporate America, then you moved up in the game like you should've. You the only nigga that I knew who would've helped

Bishop get and keep that block popping. As for the money shit, the kind of people that we'll be dealing with, we shouldn't have to come out our pockets for nothing."

From the looks on April and Blacky's faces, I could tell I wasn't the only one confused.

"Well, I know they won't just let us get it for free. Last time they gave it to us at a lower price, so I doubt it'll be much of a difference this time," I spoke.

Corn stroked his chin. "Hectic said that they would do anything to get you, right?"

"Yeah, but asking for everything to be free is asking for too much, ain't it?"

Corn shook his head no before telling me what to say to Hectic. I agreed with this, letting him know that I would do as he said but still was unclear if they would actually roll with it.

"Just think of it as they're frontin' us whatever we want. You'll pay them when it's time to reup," Corn said, making it make sense. "That way if something was to happen, it won't be you taking the L cause it'll be hard as hell for you to bounce back if we did it that way."

I nodded. "Yeah, that sounds good, getting it first and being able to sell it before paying for it, but it sounds like it can lead to problems too. What if the shit gets popped after we get it, or we go down? I'm not trying to owe nobody or have somebody at me for something I can't control or change."

"Real talk, homie. I'm only speaking on what I heard since I was copping from probably the second or third nigga that touched the shit, but it all makes sense. They need you more than you need them. So, unless they think we're on some bullshit, it shouldn't be a problem."

I shrugged. "Fuck it. I'll take your word for it. Now, let's move on to what each one of us will be doing."

"Me and Lucky will handle all the girls. I'll cook up and make sure it's always enough work to supply all the blocks," April announced.

"Keep me to what I know, let me run the joints," Blacky suggested.

"I know everybody, so if shit goes as planned, I'll deal with the niggas we sell weight to, and I'll do odd stuff as needed," Corn said, claiming his position.

I thought about what was left. "I guess that leaves me to deal with the money."

"The connect and security too," Corn said. "But Moms will help deal with the money."

"Okay, that's cool. So, I guess we need to get everybody back together. Make sure the twins come back and find as many girls as you can. I'll holla at Bull. Corn and Blacky, y'all see how many blocks we can get and get workers to work them."

"Workers will come when they hear that the block is open for business," Blacky said.

"I know, but I want someone that we can trust and who will be loyal to us, even if it's just a few. I want niggas that we can build up," I stated.

"I'll see what's up." Corn nodded.

"Tomorrow, I'm going up to Milwaukee to holla at Bull. So, let's get back together when I get back and see what we got before we talk to Hectic."

***

WHEN I CALLED BULL, he informed me that he already had plans to come to the city, which saved me a trip. He told me he would be here the next morning, and we made plans to chop it up.

I knew he was working on starting his business, and if things went as planned, it could lead him and his partner to make millions in legal money. I knew what I was going to ask him was a lot. Giving that up to play the streets again was like asking him to give up his freedom. So, if he said no, I would understand, but I would have to rethink my whole plan. I didn't let it take over my thoughts as I drove to his office. When I got off the expressway and followed the directions that Bull gave me, I didn't see anything that came off as a security firm. The building that I parked in front of looked like the rest of the warehouses around it. The only difference was that there weren't any semi-trucks coming and going. Walking up to the door, I saw a logo of the word security in the shape of an AR-15, giving me a clear indication that I was at the right place. I rang the doorbell, and a few moments later, I saw Bull walking toward the door. Once seeing that it was me, he opened the door, and we embraced like brothers.

"What's up, big timer?" I asked, looking around.

"Nothing much. What's up with you? Need me to fix somebody up for you?"

I laughed. "Naw, none of that shit. I got a little business that I want to talk about."

"That makes two of us. What's on your mind?"

Allowing him to go first, Bull began showing me around the building, a huge warehouse he'd bought to convert into a number of things. They had plans for a gun range and an indoor and outdoor training course. They even had a space for a driving course and a workout gym. The office space was the only finished area in the building, so we went there to talk. There was a waiting room with five chairs along the wall across from a reception's desk. While it was finished, the walls were plain.

"Not bad for a hood nigga. Who would have thought something like this was possible?" I said.

"Yeah, it's not bad, but my partner didn't do everything right, so I need your help."

"Just say the word and I got you," I said, knowing this business was worth investing in.

"For everything he wants, it's going to cost a lot more money than what we have, so I need a loan."

"How much?"

"That's the thing. We need a lot. We took out a loan from the bank for a quarter of a million, but that's only going to finish the building."

"Okay, but that's not telling me how much you need from me."

By the way he looked, I knew it was going to be a lot. Instead of telling me, he grabbed a piece of paper off the desk and handed it to me. I looked at it and saw everything that he needed. Cars, guns, and other gear, legal fees, and a lot of other things that added up to another quarter of a million. I tried to think of ways to get the money before I gave him an answer.

"Man, I wish you would've told me before that loan. It's going to cost more money now. I can easily give you that money, but I want it to look as legal as possible. I'll have to talk to Mama Kelly first. There's a guy who wants to buy a couple of our buildings. We weren't trying to sell them, but it's an all-cash sale, so it could go straight to you and cover everything. I think we can clear up the loan if we can make a quick sale on this house we got in the burbs."

"You'll do all that?" he asked like it was a surprise.

"Shit, why not? I'll do anything for my family, and if you ever need more, I'll get it to you. Just let me know."

"Man, Nate gon' love to hear that, but his white ass will have a bunch of questions."

"It's clean money. It ain't shit. I still got drug money I wish I could put up, but we're doing good on the legal side where it ain't no problem."

"That's what's up. Now, what business do you got?" Bull asked me.

"We are getting back in the game and want to put the team back together."

"What!? What do you mean by we? April going for that?"

"Blacky and Corn surprised me, but everybody with it," I answered.

"What about all the shit that's been going on in the streets these last few months? Is it safe?"

"It's never safe, but the Feds got who they wanted. Shit just still fucked up cause the streets is dry. Niggas going crazy cause they hungry."

"What about the connect? Who you fucking with?"

"Everybody still the same. We only need you."

"So, you want me to come back as your enforcer again?"

"Yeah, something like that."

He got quiet for a while before saying, "Man, I love you more than the lady that gave birth to me, and that's real, but it'll be stupid of me to go back to being something less than what I am now. I can't fill that position," Bull declined.

I wasn't surprised, and if it was up to me, I would call everything off, but I had everybody else to think about. I had to move on and find somebody else. Ready to leave, I stood to my feet.

"It's all good, my nigga. As much as I would love for you to be on my team, I understand your position. If I was you, I wouldn't do it either. You got a good thing going here, and I'm proud of you. Just don't be around this bitch thinking you Superman." After I was shot, Bull blamed it all on himself. No matter how much I tried letting him know it wasn't his fault, he wasn't hearing that.

"I'm Superman, nigga. Shit like this don't happen on my watch," *he would say.*

"I know I'm not Superman. I'm better than him because I'm real and trained to protect people now," he spoke, changing things up a bit.

"Bull, I know you don't want to get back in the drug game, but I need you to be a part of this some kinda way. So, what position are you willing to play?"

"You'll probably not gonna like it, but I want to be head of security and have people in play to take care of all the stuff that I used to do. My job will be to make sure you don't get so much as a scratch."

"For you to be able to do that, you'll have to be with me everywhere I go," I stated.

He laughed. "I knew you wasn't dumb."

"Hell naw, yo ass is tripping! I'm not running to be the president and don't need a secret service agent with me all day. But thinking about it, I wouldn't mind that for April."

"That's all good, but I made my offer. Take it or leave it."

I knew that it was his loyalty that made him want to protect me, and if the tables were turned, I'd probably be on the same thing.

"Alright, I'll take it, but what about this?" I asked, pointing around his office.

"I'm still going to build my business and this building into a security mecca, but you're my client now, so I'll have to find the right balance."

"Good because this shit looks too fun to give up." There was a loud noise toward the back that sounded like metal crashing onto the floor. My brows raised in expectation. "You uuuh…"

Bull waved me off. "They got it. So, when do I start?"

"I'm going to meet up with Hectic later on and let him know we're in. Hopefully, the connect will make their way up here soon. That's when I'll need you, and we'll start putting everything into motion."

"Well, my nigga, just let me know and I'll be ready for whatever," Bull assured.

"No doubt."

We shook hands.

Leaving out the building, I couldn't help but feel a sense of power and control. No drug gave me a better high than what I was feeling. The few worries I did have went to the back of my mind as I headed to meet with Hectic.

CHAPTER FOUR

Bishop

With the blocks already being clear from the Feds raiding them, Corn didn't have a problem claiming whatever blocks we wanted. After talking to Cash, he was able to get the original blocks back and the row houses on Washington and Lotus. There had been a camera installed on Lotus, but none of us cared since that wouldn't be a spot where drugs were held. Corn and Blacky also didn't have a problem finding workers either. Since niggas on the block were hungry and ready to work, they were all trying to get on our payroll.

For April, it took no work at all to get the twins. Their only question was where the weed was at. Goals accomplished, I guessed they were back at it. Aside from the twins, we only got in touch with a handful of other females because we knew the females would come pouring in once word got out, which made April's job that much easier.

I let everybody tell me of their progress before letting them know I had spoken with Bull, informing them of everything else that he brought to the team. When I told them all what I agreed to do for Bull, they brushed it off, knowing that he was worth every penny.

At the meeting with Hectic, he was on board with everything we asked for, but when he called José and Jesus, they said they would like to discuss everything in person. So, I invited them to come to Chicago.

I gave myself a week to get everything together, and finally, today was the day.

APRIL

I sat on the sectional in the family room, thinking about everything that was going on. We were finally getting back in the game, and I couldn't be happier. However, I didn't want to do any business where we laid our heads. We still had to keep a family environment for our children, so there would be no more business meetings of any sort in the public areas of our home. We didn't need our children walking in on anything we had going on. I knew that Bishop wouldn't give up his office, so I had a contractor come in and lay out a plan to gut the guest bedroom and bathroom that we had on the first floor. He also took a little off the garage and Bishop's office just to make the space big enough for everyone.

I had a custom ten-thousand-dollar mahogany table built with a hidden safe inside. I also had four mahogany chairs customized with each one of our names engraved on the back. The plush white carpet I had installed was so fluffy and soft that it felt as though you were walking on clouds while the gold and white curtains I hung from the wall gave the office a luxurious feel. There were other smaller tables along the wall, just in case there ever needed to be more than the four of us here. Bishop's office was rebuilt and connected to the boardroom and only housed a desk and chair. I wanted him to be able to put anything he wanted inside his office, so I left the decorating to him.

We all sat around the table with Bull off to the side as we planned out our day. I looked around at everyone, confused, not understanding what was going on. "Wait, so we all gon' be there? I was under the impression it would just be me and Bishop with Bull and his team."

Bishop looked at me and shrugged. "Yeah, why not?"

"Bishop, we already talked about what we want. There shouldn't be a problem, but if something changes, then we trust your judgement. There's no point in all of us being there," Corn spoke, agreeing with me.

"The point is to show them that we're one, and we stand together. That's why we all need to be there. We gotta show these niggas we a team."

"Come on, homie. That goes without saying, but that could make them uncomfortable with all of us there," Corn reasoned.

Even though I agreed with Corn, I could tell that Bishop wasn't going to change his mind, so I took his side, knowing he had his mind made up.

"Well, they already know me, and they know of you, Corn. The only new person will be Blacky, and sooner or later, they should at least get acquainted with him, so why not now?"

"If that's the way you see it, then that's what it is. So, how this gon' go?" Corn agreed, wanting to dead the conversation.

Bull stepped to the table between Corn and Blacky. "They're flying in and should be at the Joliet Airport around noon. We're going in two Sprinters. Bishop and April in one with me. They'll be there with us. It'll be enough room for a couple of their people. Y'all will be in the second one with two of my people. Bishop told me how they were on their home turf, so make them as comfortable as possible. And they can see that we're on our shit. I'm going to have a car in the front and one behind us all the way back to Chicago where you have the top floor suite at the Trump Hotel."

"Why don't we just stay in Joliet?" Blacky asked.

"That's what I forgot. Y'all need to give Bull all the blocks because we plan to give them a tour, so they can see what we're working with," Bishop informed.

"I know we got our plan, but do you see them saying no to anything?" Blacky asked, looking over at Bishop.

"Hectic was good with it, and like I said, they're willing to do whatever to work with us again. They know what we 'bout, and he already told me they need us more than we need them. So, really, they'll be fools not to give us the few things that we want. This shit happening either way, so they might as well jump on board with our request."

"What time do we leave?" Corn asked, standing from his seat at the table.

"In about two hours," Bull answered, looking down at his watch.

"Well, I'll get you them blocks then I got to go handle something real quick," Corn spoke, looking over to Bull.

"Alright, everybody. Do what needs to be done but be back here well before the official meetup time. I'm not tryna be late."

Everybody got up and shook hands before walking out the door, leaving me alone with Bishop.

"You don't have nothing to do, baby?" I asked.

"Not now but I gotta take the kids to Mama Kelly's. I'm going to get them up soon and get them ready. What about you?"

"The twins should be here soon. They want to know what they'll be doing. I told them we need them for other reasons now."

"They ass gon' be okay with it if they can start back smoking weed. How you feel about everything going on? You cool with it?" Bishop asked, looking into my eyes. I could tell he was looking for me to lie, so I told the truth.

"No. I don't have a problem with the plan and us getting back into the game."

"But you got a problem with something, so tell me what it is. Talk to me, baby."

"This bullshit about me having a fake ass bodyguard with me all the time and the fact that it's a bitch. Fuck that! Like what the fuck, Bishop? We ain't never been on no shit like that. I don't need no other bitch protecting me."

Bishop laughed. "You kiss your kids with that mouth? I could get a dude to be with you if that's really what you want."

"Fuck you, John! I don't need nobody with me."

"Well, that's not something you have a choice on, so you might as well get used to the idea like I had to. We all have a bodyguard, April, not just you. Is there anything that I can do to make it better for you?"

"Well, I don't know if you can make it happen, but I've been wanting one of them dogs like Bull got. I'll pay whatever to have one."

"Don't trip. I got you."

The doorbell rang, and I got up to answer it. "That must be the twins. I'll go and let you do Daddy duties but bring my babies to me before you leave. Got to make sure they know Mommy loves them." I smiled.

"I got you but make sure you show me how much you love me too."

"When you get me that dog, I might show you a thing or two." I walked over to him and kissed him before going to answer the door.

"What's up with y'all bust downs?" I teased the twins as they came in and hugged me.

"Don't do us, April. You know very few niggas can get some of these goods."

"So, y'all let them few just hit it at the same time, huh?"

They both looked at each other and started laughing. "Bitch, who told you about that?" Jayla asked, still laughing.

"I don't give up my sources but just know I know about y'all nasty asses."

"Girl, don't front on us. We got paid, plus all three of them niggas knew how to lay the pipe." They gave each other a high five and then started making a money sign with their fingers.

"Oh, so y'all selling pussy now? If so, I can be y'all pimp," I joked.

"Naw, bitch, it ain't that kind of party. Them niggas was up in the club acting like they was God's gift to women, talking about can't no one woman last a night with one of them, so I told them I'd put all three of them to sleep if they put their money where their mouths was. What they didn't know was we were switching on them till they tapped out," Kayla revealed.

"So, how much money y'all get?"

The twins smiled. "A lady never tells," Jayla answered.

"Whatever. Y'all still some hoes, but let's go handle this business because I got to go soon."

"Damn, bitch. You gon' rush us like that? What you ain't got time for us no more, Miss Queen Pin?" Jayla continued.

"Naw, boo. I'm only the princess right now, but before it's over, I'll be the queen. You better believe that."

"You tryna say Bishop finally gon' marry you?" Kayla shot back, clearly throwing shade.

"I would've been had that nigga's name. Yo ass playin' games," Jayla spoke.

"I don't need no piece of paper to tell me where me and my man stand. His ass ain't going nowhere, and if he tries, I bet he won't have a dick to fuck another bitch with."

We went in the kitchen and sat at the table. I didn't want nobody else to see the boardroom until it was fully done, and I wanted to see my babies before they left, so the kitchen would have to do.

"If we're not going to be doing what we do best, then what y'all want us to do?" Jayla asked.

I looked at both of them. "Well, we really can find anyone to bag up."

"No one that's faster and can be trusted like us."

"True, but even if y'all was to do it, we'll still need more hands. I just hope enough money can keep whoever we get honest. Everybody else is stepping up, and we think y'all can do better for us doing what y'all do now. We're going to have a ton of money coming in, and even though Bishop likes touching all of it, he had to admit we'll need somebody that we can trust to handle our money." I looked at them both, wanting them to know that I was serious about what I was telling them.

"We got a lawyer that's going to handle our legal stuff, so we need somebody that will work with him, especially when somebody gets locked up," I continued.

"So, in other words, we're still going to be working a nine to five?" The look on Jayla's face was filled with disappointment.

"I guess but not really because you'll be working with the lawyer. Kayla will only be there for that if y'all really need her and only when he needs you. Kayla, if you can do everything that we need, then I'm sure Bishop won't care where you do it at."

"And how much money is we getting paid?" Kayla asked, giving a bit of attitude.

"Mommy!" Jasmine and Rose called out in unison, entering the room in a full sprint.

I switched to mommy mode in a split second as they came running over to me.

"How's Mommy's babies doing?" I hugged and kissed each of them.

"Daddy said if we got finished fast enough, we can eat breakfast at McDonald's." Rose looked up at Bishop. "Right, Daddy?"

"That's right, baby," he replied.

"Well, did Daddy tell you that you're going to McDonald's no matter how fast you got ready?"

"You saying that Daddy tricked us?" Rose asked.

"He sure did, baby, but you want to know how to get him back?"

"Yeah, because I don't like to be tricked," Jasmine said.

"I don't like it too, Mommy," Rose spoke.

"Tell Daddy he gotta take y'all to McDonald's for breakfast and lunch," I said.

"Yay! We get to go to McDonald's two times! Thank you, Mommy!" Rose jumped up and down, clapping her hands.

"You know us girls got to stick together. Now, give me a kiss so I can see my favorite boy." They both kissed me before running over to talk to the twins. I got up and grabbed Junior from Bishop. He couldn't talk yet, but he gave me a big smile after I gave him a few kisses. I fixed his clothes before handing him back.

Bishop shifted Junior in his arms. "You want me to bring you something back, traitor?"

"Yeah, just grab a few breakfast sandwiches." I turned to the twins. "Everything straight with y'all?"

"Yeah, we're good."

"What's good, y'all?" Bishop asked, looking over at the twins.

"Hey, Bishop," they both said.

"Alright, girls. It's time to go." Bishop headed toward the door with Jasmine and Rose following close behind.

"Bye, Mommy. Love you," they both said before walking out the door.

"Love y'all too. Make sure y'all help with your brother." I waited until they were gone before sitting back down and getting back to business.

"Where were we at?" I asked.

"Money," both said at once.

"Okay. How much do y'all get paid now?"

"I get fifty-two hundred a month, but I work a lot of overtime," Jayla said.

"And I get four grand a month," Kayla answered.

"How much do y'all think is fair?"

"Whatever you say." Jayla shrugged.

"Yeah, we know you won't play us," Kayla agreed.

"Me and Bishop talked about it, and he said to double your pay. We'll pay ten thousand to start and see how everything goes. Then, we'll revisit this conversation in the next six months. Maybe even slide y'all some bonuses here and there."

"That's a deal!" Kayla said.

"She speaks for herself. I want one more thing," Jayla stated, looking over at me.

"And what's that?" I asked, not knowing what else she could want.

"I need free weed whenever I want. I know y'all about to have that good shit." She laughed.

"We can do that for you," I agreed.

"Yeah, I want that too." Kayla tried to hop on her sister's bandwagon.

"Naw, you already said deal," I said, fucking with her, knowing that she was going to get weed too.

"You sure did." Jayla laughed.

"Damn, who side is you on?" Kayla questioned her twin with a mug on her face.

"The bitch that's going to pay me."

Kayla crossed her arms and shrugged with a smile. "Don't trip. I'll just act like I'm you."

"You can't fool me," I said.

"I bet you can't tell me right now which I am. The whole time you've been talking to both of us because you don't know if I'm the one that works with the lawyer or the money."

She had me on that, but I still had a fifty-fifty chance of guessing right. "Bet something then."

"I'll put my first month's pay up you won't get it right."

"You're the lawyer one," I guessed, looking at the other twin, who shook her head. "Fuck! Get out of my house."

"Bring me my money first, and next time, you better get it right," Kayla said with a smile.

"Fuck you. I'll bring the money. You just gonna give it right back to me buying weed." I laughed.

CHAPTER FIVE

Bishop

WE GOT TO THE AIRPORT, WAITING ABOUT FIVE MINUTES BEFORE I SAW the jet coming in to land. When they flew us to Mexico, they put us in a nice private jet, but the one they came in was on another level. It was like the Bugatti of jets. As I watched it roll down the runway, I vowed to myself that one day, I was going to take my family on a trip in one of those — no matter how much it cost.

It was a beautiful day, and the sun was shining brightly, which was rare for November. When José stepped out the jet, he turned his face up to the sky for a few seconds before coming down the stairs. Soon after, Jesus followed, and seeing them standing side by side, I couldn't help laughing.

"Be nice," April whispered, hitting my arm.

"Fuck that, look at what these niggas wearing." I watched as they both stood there in lime green suits with rhinestones all over them. Bull laughed from the driver's seat, knowing what I was saying was true.

"While y'all talking shit, I bet if y'all had the money they did, y'all ass would put them suits on too, hats and all." April laughed.

"I might be in a suit, but it won't be lime green, and it damn sure wouldn't have no fuckin' rhinestones on it," I said. shaking my head before exiting the car.

"How was the trip here?" I asked, walking up to José and Jesus, shaking both their hands.

"Oh, it was good, but I didn't expect Chicago to be so nice this time of the year," José answered.

"How many times do I have to tell you that we're not in Chicago yet?" Jesus asked, looking over at José.

"It's close enough," José replied. They both began saying a few words in Spanish while April and I looked at each other. Neither of us understood anything they were saying.

"Don't mind my brother. He's clearly not the brains behind this operation. Good thing the ladies don't want him for his brains." José laughed.

I wanted to let him know they didn't want them for their sense of style either, but instead, I asked if they brought bodyguards with them.

Jesus raised up both of his eyebrows. "Bodyguards? We are guests in your home. You are our bodyguards."

I nodded my head, letting him know they were both safe. He was correct. They were our guests, so we would ensure nothing happened to them while they were here.

Jesus acknowledged April standing beside me, shaking her hand before turning back to me. "Where is Hectic at? I thought he'd be here too."

"He's checking us into the hotel now. We gonna meet him there." We got in the Sprinter and made small talk as we rode back to the city.

Our tour of the block was my first time on them. Since I wasn't the one who handled them, there was no need for me to come to them until now. More than a few were off the e-way, which made it easier for the white customers from the suburbs to get what they wanted and get back home easily instead of riding to the middle of the hood.

We weren't talking business as we rode around. I was mainly listening to them comment about certain things they were seeing. I looked out the window as we pulled up to a red light. I didn't know what made me focus on the lady walking past. She wore a knee length coat that looked as though she'd taken it from two-week-old garbage. Her hair was dirty and matted, and I could tell she hadn't showered in weeks. She looked nothing like the woman I once knew, but I still recognized her.

I got Bull's attention and pointed at her. "Aye, have somebody in the last car get that lady for me." I let the window down. "Mama T!"

She looked up from the ground and turned my way. She just stared at me for a few seconds. "Who is that?"

"Mama T, it's John."

"John?" She looked like she was high and really didn't know who I was. "My son's old friend?"

"Yeah."

The light turned green as one of Bull's men walked toward her. I let her know to get in the car with him and he'd follow me.

She did just that, and I let the window back up. No one said anything, but knowing who she was, April nodded. We couldn't blame her for what Lil Tone did.

Arriving at the hotel, I sent everyone up to the room, telling them that I'd be up in a few minutes. I had one of Bull's men stay with me and went to the other car to talk to Mama T.

I opened the back passenger door and leaned down to get a better look at her. "I've been looking for you... where you been?"

She shrugged. "Around. I called you but never could reach you, so I gave up."

"Yeah, that's probably when I got shot and was in jail for a while."

"Well, it doesn't look like you're doing all that bad now. Let me get a few dollars so I can get something to eat."

"Do you still smoke crack, or do you do something else?"

"Crack is my new son, and I won't stop until I'm back with my other son."

I stood tall and released a heavy sigh, shaking my head at her words. I leaned back inside. "Where you live at?"

She was rocking back-and-forth, and I could tell she was high and wanted more.

She answered me. "Wherever I can find. Sometimes with a friend, on the train, and if I have to, on the streets. It really doesn't matter to me as long as I am high. When I'm high, I don't feel shit, and that's how I like it."

"How about I get you a room for the night, so you can eat some real food, get some sleep, and tomorrow, I'll get you a place to stay? You can clean up, and then, I'll give you some money for yourself."

Mama T's eyes got big. "How much?"

"Enough, but you need to start taking care of yourself again. You don't look like yo self anymore, and that's fucked up."

"Can I get something to smoke right now?"

"I don't have none, but I can get you something to drink.

"Take her to the store and get her some new clothes. Then, take her to one of the motels in the hood and stay with her tonight," I spoke, turning to one of the guards.

"I'll have to check in with Bull first," he replied.

"Don't worry about that. I'll have him call you."

I didn't have much money on me, so I gave him a debit card, giving him the pin before heading upstairs. Everybody was sitting around, eating, and I didn't realize how hungry I was until I sat down and started eating myself.

When we were done, everyone made their way to the living room area. A taupe C-shaped sectional sat in the middle of the room, and we all took our seats. An ice bucket that housed several bottles of champagne sat on a glass coffee table in front of the sectional. We each grabbed a glass, and Jesus poured champagne into each of them. I wasn't sure if it was meant to be a silent toast, but he sat down, drinking from his glass without saying a word. Everyone else followed suit, drinking from their glasses as well.

"The whole family is here this time. Last time, Mister Corn wasn't in the best situation, and Blacky was a soldier. But today... we sat down and ate and drank as equals with the same goal. So, I welcome you both into my family's embrace," Jesus spoke in a low voice. Blacky nodded, and Corn raised his glass toward them. "My friends, Bishop and April... thank you for the opportunity to once again do business."

Before I had a chance to say anything, José started talking. "Hectic told us about the things your team asked for. We're willing to do what it takes to meet your terms, but we don't think it's a good idea. However," he held his hand up, palm facing us, to halt any unexpected outburst, "rather than simply saying no, I'll give you the reason why we don't think it's the best move for either of us. Hopefully, you agree, and we can come up with a better solution." He looked at Hectic, who was sitting closest to Jesus. "Are you willing to come back and stay in this area like they want you to?"

"I don't have a problem with it," he replied.

"Even though your pay will be cut in half with this position?"

Hectic shrugged. "I'll feel better if I was dealing with them rather than someone else."

"Okay, that's done. Now, Bishop. Do you believe in learning from your mistakes?" Jesus asked, now looking over at me.

"The ones that I made, I try not to make them again, so yeah."

"That's good. I feel everyone should feel that way. If we agree to give you the exclusive privilege of being the only ones to sell our product in Chicago, or the west side, then we might be making the same mistake that just cost us millions. We don't need any of the people that already work for us getting wind of the business we have with you. That could cause a problem that we don't need to have," Jesus spoke.

Just like the other times that I met them, Jesus picked up where José left off. "We want you more behind the scenes. We want to give you a few guys to work under your team's supervision. That way when they contact Hectic with the order, he only has to deal with you, and once you put everything together, you tell them where it goes, and you have no contact with any outsiders. While we hope it never happens, our people know the repercussions that come with being a rat, and they know how we treat those who stay loyal."

He stopped talking for a few seconds, but this time, I knew he had more to say, so I stayed quiet and waited for him to continue. "Most of the people that didn't get caught in that raid and want to do business are scared of Chicago right now. This will probably be for a while, but Chicago is the safest place. The Feds have everybody, and the D.A. is focused on prosecuting them. So, it's really on you to set the distraction platform."

I was caught up trying to keep up with what they were saying and how it would fit into our plan when Corn spoke up. "That's pretty much what we want."

"But there might be a time when someone else wants to come this way, and we welcome it and won't stop it," José responded back.

"We don't need much time if that's the case, but will they have the same resources to compete with us?"

"This leads me to our next point. We know Bishop is great with the business on his own. So, we have faith that with all of you together, a master plan has been put in motion that will benefit your family, and we respect that. However, we need it to be understood that Bishop works for us. We can offer cocaine at three thousand per kilo, which is nine thousand less than anybody else. For each kilo of heroin, you'll only pay ten thousand. Do I even have to tell you what kind of deal that is? And since Bishop will be working for us, we'll pay for his time, so how does five percent of each sale sound?"

"It sounds good to me." I knew a good deal when I heard one.

"Yeah, everything sounds good except I didn't hear nothing about weed," April added.

José had a sly grin as he looked at April. "Oh, I forgot about that. For you, April, we'll give you that at no cost if you'll get these guys to agree."

"Then I don't think we got nothing else to say at this point. We got everything we want and then some," April replied.

Jesus held out his hands. "So, we got a deal?"

We were so excited that we agreed, but Blacky spoke at the last second. "What about the payment? How will that work?"

José cleared his throat. "Yes, that won't be a problem at all. How about we settle the difference at the end of each month?"

José and Jesus began shaking our hands. Once finished, Jesus began speaking again. "We're still going to be here tomorrow. Let's meet up for lunch and hang out? It's been a long time since we've been somewhere to have fun, and unlike back home, no one knows us. So, while we're in the Chi-town, we want to do something."

Not really one to run the streets, I drew a blank. "Like what?"

"A club or something," José said. "Maybe a strip club?"

I looked at Corn. "Bro, you know more about that than I do. Set it up."

"I got it. Don't trip." Corn smiled.

"April, maybe you can bring some of your friends to be our dates. We never been with a Black girl before." Jesus smiled.

Everyone laughed.

"I got the perfect girls for y'all," April said. "You need one too, Hectic?"

"Since you offered, I won't turn it down." He laughed.

"We're looking forward to it. What time should we be ready?" José asked.

Corn looked at his watch, and his brows creased. Nodding slowly, he looked back up. "Let's have a late lunch. We'll be here to get y'all at one."

José and Jesus agreed, and I clasped my hands together. "I'm going to have a couple of my people stay around. If y'all need something or want to go somewhere, just let me know."

Bull was the only security that was in the suite, and he stayed back in the cut. I called him over and explained that I sent one of his guys with Mama T, then I told him that I needed him to personally stay with the brothers and have a few of his men too. I was surprised that he didn't argue about staying with me.

On the ride home, I tried to think of all the numbers for everything but gave up, knowing money wasn't going to be an issue. We were going to make way more than we could count, and this time, I was going to enjoy it.

The next day, I started early by going shopping. April brought the twins and Baby D to spend the day with us. Baby D was April's best friend, but she was doing her own thing, so anytime they could get together, they were ready to act a fool.

When we got to the hotel to pick up José and Jesus, Hectic was already there, and they were in the middle of a conversation. They were speaking in Spanish, so none of us understood a word they were saying. Or so I thought until Baby D started laughing.

April grabbed her arm, but it was too late, all three of them turned to her. They all spoke at the same time. "What?"

Surprising everybody in the room, she started talking to them in Spanish. They was going back-and-forth. I knew that I was confused until Baby D turned to us. "Hectic is trying to explain to them that nobody dresses like that here, and I told them that they'll stand out in the worst way." Today, they were wearing white, green, and red suits. They looked like they were there on their way to the North Pole to make toys.

Hectic started waving his hands. "That's not the worst of it, turn around and let them see the back of your jackets." When they did, there were skulls on both of them. Continuing his point, Hectic said, "Skulls are popular in our culture, but can y'all tell them that people will look at them like they're stupid, especially going to the strip club tonight?"

I decided to put my two cents in and stop everything. "How about we just go shoppin'? We went this morning and should've came to get y'all. The ladies can help y'all get something slick."

Of the three of us guys, we all had different styles. Corn was wearing blue jeans and a tight black shirt. I always got on him about the tight shirts he wore, but he only joked back that he'd gotten bigger since he bought it. Blacky turned into a skinny jean wearing nigga and had on a Polo shirt. I went with white pants, button up shirt, and a white Chicago Sox fitted hat turned to the back.

I didn't know how the ladies did it, but they came to show out. April had on just enough for me not to get mad. She was rocking a white dress that stopped at mid-thigh with a strap holding it around her neck. We all did a double take when the twins stepped out. I caught Corn looking at their asses a few times, and I couldn't blame him; they were curvy and thick in all the right places. April said that they'd glowed up. They had on the same skirt and shirt that had a slit between their breasts, but they made it easy for us to tell them apart. Kayla had on red and Jayla black. They also had the same hairstyle, a long, blonde weave. Baby D was wearing a light pink bodysuit. It was so tight that I didn't know how she got in it, and I swore you could see all her business.

April cleared her throat. "Maybe Hectic need to change too."

Hectic turned toward April. "Hold up, April. I thought we was cool. What's wrong with my clothes?" He looked down and brushed his shirt off with his hands like there was lent on it.

The brothers laughed at Hectic before April could answer. "I mean, nothing is really wrong with it, but every time I see you, it's the same style, a V-neck and jeans. I bet you got a zip-hoodie somewhere. At least switch it up for tonight."

He nodded. "Okay, that's fair. I thought you was saying my clothes wasn't right but forget all that. Which one of these ladies do I have the honor of spending the night with?"

Jesus said something in Spanish, but Kayla cut him off. "Can we get English or a translator? I don't want y'all biddin' on me or plannin' to kidnap me."

"Now that you mentioned it, how about it? Or you can come on your own." Jesus looked her up and down as if giving it real thought.

Kayla gave a nervous laugh. "Flattering but will you settle for the night?" She walked over to him and grabbed his arm in a hug.

Jayla went to José's side, leaving Hectic with Baby D, but from the look in his eyes, he didn't mind at all.

We left the hotel and hit the stores downtown til we found outfits they were good with. It was still suits but just with a vest and a black and white button-down shirt for the brothers, and Hectic went with jeans and button up shirt. They got on him because he was matching me.

By the time we got done, it was four o'clock, and the restaurant we made reservations for gave our reservation away due to us being late. Thankfully, Baby D had a friend that worked at an Applebee's not too far from where we were, making it easy to get a table there. When we got our table, we got the party started. José and Jesus were all into the twins, and they were eating the attention up. Before the food got to us, we were already two shots in. I stuck to what I knew, getting Hennessey while everybody else had shit I'd never heard of. We stayed longer than normal, receiving several stares from the tables around us. We were loud but were sure to leave a nice tip.

We all got in one of the black Sprinters with Bull driving. In the other Sprinter was the security team. Being that the club wouldn't be bussing for a couple more hours and the Sprinter had its own bar, the twins, being the life of the party, started by pouring everybody shots and rolling up blunts.

Kayla reached over me and handed one to April. "I don't care what Bishop gotta say. We gettin' high, bitch." I took the blunt from April, and Kayla damn near jumped in my lap trying to get it back. "Come on, Bishop, this gon' be one of the last nights to kick it. Let her smoke with us."

"Fuck lettin' her hit it. Yo ass need to take a blunt to the head. It just might loosen you up some," Jayla added.

I put the blunt in my mouth. "At least one of y'all fuck with me. Let's put this shit in the air."

Corn shook his head. "Hell naw. Y'all not about to turn my boy out. Get that blunt from him."

"I second that. You can't have him smoking what he selling," Hectic said, living up to what he always told me.

I laughed as I grabbed the lighter from Kayla and lit the blunt. I took a hit and blew it out. "Thankfully, I ain't got shit to do with sellin' weed cause I'm about to have some fun tonight."

Blacky was sitting on the other side of me, and after I took another hit, he reached across the space. "Let me get that. If you cuttin' up, then you best believe I am too, my nigga."

When we got the weed in rotation, Kayla hooked her phone up to the Sprinter's Bluetooth and put some music on while we drove around. By the time we pulled up to the club, we were already feeling ourselves.

The parking lot was packed, and there was a long line outside. I could tell it was a little hood spot, but I still felt comfortable. I had Bull and his boys by my side, but everyone I saw looked like they were only there to have a good time.

All eyes was on us as we got out as close to the entrance as possible. Walking past the people waiting in line, we heard them say that we were either rappers, singers, or played every sport that was heard of. Some of the security team did look like they belonged on the offensive line for the Bears, so that made sense.

Corn led the way, and when we got to the front door, he said something to the bouncer, who let us right in, causing some of the people in line to yell out. We walked into a hall lit with black lights. There was a thick ass stripper there waiting on us. She led us in a door and up some stairs to the VIP section. We had a view overlooking all three stages, so we would be able to watch all the dancers as they performed. There was a stripper pole in the middle of the VIP section with black leather couches and glass tables on all four sides.

The brothers sat with the twins on one couch; me, April, Baby D, and Hectic sat across from them, and Blacky and Corn took the other two couches by themselves. Bull positioned one of his guys at the door we came into and another one at each of the two sets of stairs leading down to the club where I was sure the other four were.

The stripper that led us up to VIP asked us how many of the girls did we want, and before she could finish her sentence, Jesus yelled that he wanted them all. Everybody laughed, and she said that she'd have a group come up every thirty minutes. I remembered how April got the other time we went to the strip club in Mexico, so I couldn't wait to see what tonight was going to bring.

April had gone and gotten five thousand worth of fives before we came. We sat down, and the owner came over with a bag. He introduced himself, dumped stacks of ones on each of the tables, and motioned for the girls following him toward each one of us. They were each carrying a bucket with a bottle inside.

Corn let us know that this was only the first twenty thousand, a gift from Mama Kelly, telling us to have fun, but another twenty thousand was ready after the first was gone. We tried to talk them out of it, but Jesus, José, and Hectic said they wanted to each put up twenty too. They said they'd make it back in five minutes. April tapped me, and I knew what she was thinking. I gave the owner five debit cards with ten thousand on each. Fuck it, we were going to enjoy this shit.

Everybody grabbed a bottle and popped them open. I just took a sip, but seeing that everybody else was downing their shit, I followed suit.

April led all the females that came with us down to the dance floor, leaving just the guys up there as the first wave of strippers came in. We all grabbed a stack of money, and from there, it seemed like every time I looked up, there was a new ass on me. Girls were on the pole, and girls were dancing on each other. Just as our girls were coming back up, everybody started yelling. I looked up to see the brothers looking over the rail at the stage below us and throwing money. It was raining all over the stage.

Every hour, there was a new bag of money, fresh drinks, and more strippers. Everybody was having fun.

Bull wouldn't drink or let his guys drink, but we made sure, before we left, that he got a dance from all the strippers. Then, we went to the regular dance floor and took turns dancing with the ladies.

April and I chose our room and retired for the night. Closing the door, she gave me the best strip show of the night, and everything that followed had to be one of the best nights for both of us. The sun was up long before we actually went to sleep.

CHAPTER SIX

April

"Baby, you woke?" I asked softly as I laid beside Bishop.

"Don't think I got any sleep and it'll probably be a few days before sleep even crosses my mind again." Bishop rolled over and kissed my lips. "What about you?"

Yesterday, the very first big shipment came in, and today, we had to make sure we supplied everyone that got product from us. It had been three months since we made the deal with José and Jesus, and we'd been slowly putting work out to get the traffic moving on our blocks. Now, we planned to flood the streets, so we could put everything into full gear.

"Boy, after what you did to me last night, I'm surprised I woke up this early. I don't know what that was about, but you must be really excited or nervous because you let it all out last night."

"Maybe a bit of both, but I wouldn't say I let it all out. If I didn't have to get these kids ready and drop Jasmine off at school, I'd be ready for more. What you got going on?"

I looked at the clock and saw we didn't have time to do anything, so I answered him. "Well, I cooked up a few bricks yesterday, and I want to do a few more today and over the weekend so that we always have them. Lucky and Mona are gonna watch over everything getting bagged up and package everything up for Blacky to pick up."

"I need you to make some time to go talk to Bull. He said he got something important that he needs one of us to deal with, and I need to handle a few things with Hectic before everybody meets like you want us to," he spoke.

"I can do that. I want to see the finished building anyways so do you. I'll go fix breakfast and get your clothes ready." He kissed me before rolling out of bed and putting some shorts on. I waited until he was gone before I called Mama Kelly.

"You ready for me to come pick the babies up?" she asked.

"Not yet, but I want to make sure that everything is set up like it should be."

She smacked her lips. "Girl, when have you known me not to get something right? I'll be there at 3:30 with everything set up just like you want, so don't worry."

I knew she was right, but I was nervous. "I'm sorry. I just want it to be perfect."

"Trust me, honey… it'll be a lot better than you think."

"Okay, I have to go cook, but I'll see you later." I hung up then laid Bishop's clothes out on the bed. If he had a say so, he would walk around like he was still working the block. After a while, he gave in, and I started buying him button-up shirts and jeans that fit him. The only thing he wouldn't let me buy for him was his shoes and hats. Bishop had a collection so big, they almost needed their own room.

I went downstairs to begin cooking breakfast, and moments later, Bishop brought Rose and Junior down. "I think Jasmine is sick, so she's not going to school, and I don't want her to go to the daycare. Can she ride with you?"

"What's wrong with her?" I asked in concern.

"Just a headache and her temperature is 101.3. I gave her some medicine and told her I'll bring her some breakfast up, so she can rest some more."

"Yeah, she'll have to be with me then."

I took Junior from Bishop and put him in his chair then helped Rose into hers before going back to cooking and making everybody a plate. Fifteen minutes later, Bishop was back to get his and Jasmine's plates.

Not having to drop Jasmine off, Bishop decided to drop the kids off at Mama Kelly's, and I got ready for what I knew was going to be a long day. Before getting Jasmine up, I called Bull to see if it was a good time for me to come see him, and when he said yeah, we left.

Pulling up to the building, I was surprised at how big it was. After they got the money, it only took a little over a month for them to finish the building.

I had to get buzzed in, but Bull met me before I got to his office. "What's good, sis?"

"Life." I gave him a hug and stepped back to fix his tie. "I like this suit thing. I wish that I could get Bishop to wear something like this, but I'll give him a bowtie instead. But what's up with you?"

"Nothing much, just tryin' to make a lil more outta life. But you must be crazy if you think I'm wearin' this shit by choice. Nate wants us to look professional, so unless the job calls for somethin' different, we have to wear black suits and ties, which I'm not feelin' at all. Hell, I can barely put the damn thing on. We already talked about the bowtie, but the Nation of Islam does that, and we don't wanna be confused with them. But as to why you're here, I got something that I think you'll like."

"What is it?" I asked, perplexed.

"We gotta go out south to pick it up. You want to ride with me or drive yourself?"

I made a face, and he started laughing. He knew I didn't like riding with him.

"I'll follow you but don't be driving all fast and shit."

"I need to teach you how to drive just in case something was to happen, and you need to get out a jam," Bull suggested.

I knew he was right, but for now, I just got in my car and followed him. It only took us twenty minutes to get there, and right away, I knew I was getting the dog I asked for. The building was brick and set back like a warehouse, but it wasn't the building that gave it away. Before I opened the car door, the smell hit me. If Jasmine wasn't sick, she would've been on her own because I was so excited that I practically had to drag her to keep up.

Bull led the way into the building, and there were cages of dogs everywhere. I looked at each dog to see which one would be mine.

A guy came out of a side room. "Bull, what's going on? Are these the young ladies that we're getting a dog today?"

"Yeah, this is April and my niece, Jasmine," Bull introduced.

"Okay, April, do you know what breed you want?"

I was looking around and saw all kinds of dogs. "I want one just like he's got." I pointed at Bull.

"Okay, so a pit bull. How about a color?"

I scrunched my lips to the side and shrugged. "I don't know."

"Well, follow me and I'll let you see what we have." He walked toward the back, and we followed close behind. "If you want to leave with the dog today, you have to pick from the ones on the right. They're trained and ready to go. The ones on the left still need some work, but we can fast-track things if you want one of those," the man informed.

"Naw, I want to leave with one today." I didn't know how I was going to pick since I wanted them all.

Jasmine grabbed my hand. "Mommy, I want this one." I looked at the one she pointed to, an all-white pit bull.

"Let Mommy look at the other ones first and maybe we'll get that one."

"You pick yours, and I pick mine. I want this one." I thought about it, called Bishop, and immediately regretted it, remembering that he was with Hectic.

I didn't hang up since I knew he'd just call back. He picked up on the second ring. "I'm sorry, baby, but since I got you on the phone, thank you for the dog."

"Hectic knew that you were going to call, and you're welcome. You said you wanted one, so that's what you get."

"Well, since Jasmine is with me, she now wants a dog too."

"Did the one she pick match the name?" he asked.

"Huh?" I asked, confused.

"She wants to name her dog Lady."

I finally caught on. "She not sick, is she?"

"No." He laughed. "But you would've known something was up,

so I had to play it off. I wanted you to take Lil John and Rose, but you really would've known, so I got Amanda taking them," Bishop revealed.

"Boy, bye." I turned to Jasmine. "You sure that's the one you want, baby?"

"Yes, Mommy. She's so pretty."

"Well, let's make sure it's a she before we get it. You don't want a boy dog named Lady." I laughed. The guy heard me, went and opened the cage, and rolled the dog over. Thankfully, it was a female.

I looked down at Jasmine. "You know you have to feed her?"

She cut me off. "Clean up after her, wash her, and walk her. Daddy told me if I don't take care of her, I will lose her. I know."

"Well, didn't you two come up with the master plan to keep this from me?"

"Sorry, Mommy."

"It's okay, baby. Are there any more secrets you're keeping from me?" I asked, now wanting to know everything.

"Mommy, if it's a secret, then I can't tell you." Jasmine smiled.

I knew it was something when she dismissed me by playing with her new dog.

I finally picked a light brown one that had a white spot on her chest which resembled a heart. I wanted to know if they were going to protect and do what I saw Bull's dogs do. The guy said that after some training, we'd know how to control them.

He gave us everything we needed to learn more about each dog and set us up for training every Saturday. All that, Bishop had already paid for.

As we were leaving, Bull stopped us. "On Monday, me and my sister are coming, and we'll be there as long as you and Bishop are in the hood or taking care of business. She can follow you or be in the car with you. It really doesn't matter because she'll blend in."

———

LATER THAT DAY, I met his sister, Miracle. She would trick somebody real quick with her looks if they didn't know that she was trained to put shit down like her brother. I knew that with us together, niggas and bitches would be intimidated. She was a couple inches taller than me with coffee brown skin and long, curly hair that stopped in the middle of her back. We kicked it for a little, and the only thing I wasn't feeling was how she dressed, so as she left, I gave her ten thousand to go shopping with. I had to have her looking the part.

Since we had some time, I took Jasmine to the pet store, so we could get everything she needed for her new dog. Of course, she got everything pink for hers, and I grabbed some random stuff as well. We got home and waited for everybody as we read the papers about feeding times, how often to groom them, and how to keep them fit.

I HAD a surprise set up for everybody and told them to be at our house before 3:30 p.m. The twins didn't have much to do yet, and anytime they knew one of us would be home, they showed up. Today was no different, and they showed up early.

Hectic was able to get Jayla a job working with the lawyer that did Bishop's case, and Kayla quit her job and shared the office with Bishop at our house, so she could work on investing and cleaning up some of our money through the stock market and other businesses. She even got Bull to let her work as the accountant for his business.

I opened the door, and Kayla saw my dog and ran off, screaming so loudly I knew my neighbors heard her.

"That bitch don't do dogs, girl," Jayla informed, falling over laughing.

"Well, she better get used to it. This one here will be with me all the time, but she's nice. Just put your hand out and let her come to you and smell you." That was what the paper said to do to get people comfortable with the dog, so I tested it out.

Jayla stuck her hand out, and the dog smelled it and licked it before coming back to my side. She turned and yelled to her sister. "Girl, this dog is nice. Stop being so damn scared."

Kayla was damn near at our front gate and turned to yell. "Ain't no such thing as a nice dog if it got teeth. Tell her to take that ugly thing somewhere else."

I laughed at her. "You better watch how you talk about my baby. Matter fact, just because you called her ugly, I'm going to name her Beauty. And since she isn't going anywhere, I guess I only have one twin working for me now," I spoke.

"Don't play with me, April! That thing better not bite me!" She came back, watching Beauty the whole way. She attempted to pass by on the other side, and I barked at her. She damn near jumped out of her skin. "April! Stop playing. I'm scared of them things."

"Be nice to her or she'll eat your ass up," I said, joking with her.

"You lucky I need this money. I'll pretend it's not there. So, what's going on? When can I start getting paid?"

"Next month but I can give you something now if you need it."

Jayla's brows raised. "That bitch don't need no money, girl."

"That's where you're wrong, Jayla. I want to start saving for a car."

I held up a finger to stop the conversation from going any further. "We can talk about business later. Right now, me and Jasmine are learning about our dogs. Do what y'all want while we wait for everybody else to get here."

"She has one of those beasts too?" Kayla asked, looking around the room for Jasmine's dog.

"Of course. Her daddy bought her one."

"Well, I guess I lost a niece." Kayla laughed.

They went about their day, and I got back to what I was doing until Lucky, Blacky, Corn, and Baby D arrived. Bishop came in, and Mama Kelly called to say everything would be set up in five minutes. I got everybody in the living room and told Jasmine to let Mama Kelly in when she got there.

When everybody sat down, Bishop stood up from his chair and told me to sit down. Even though it was rude since this was my meeting, I sat down on the arm of his chair, hoping that he wouldn't take too long and mess up my surprise.

I wanted to say something but let him finish. "Now, a few months ago, I heard something that wasn't meant for my ears, but it got me thinkin' bout how good my woman is to me. She deals with the shit that y'all don't see plus the shit everybody can see. She's a ride or die female. To top that off, she gave birth to three of my kids and is a second mother to my other two. So, before we get started on this next phase, I want to say thank you and I love you, baby," Bishop spoke.

I couldn't believe what I was hearing. I knew he loved me, but he showed it through actions more than words.

"Awww," the women present said simultaneously. The tears cascading down their cheeks told me that I wasn't the only one moved by his speech.

"I love you too, baby."

Blacky stood. "Well, he ain't the only one that loves his girl. I just don't know how to be that soft to say all that."

Even I had to laugh through my tears. Lucky pulled him down and hit him on the head.

"Don't trip, Blacky. It took me three months to get that perfect. It's all good though. They're going to forget everything I said and what you want to say, but what we're about to do, they'll never forget." Bishop sat down, so I thought he was done.

I stood back up just in time as Mama Kelly and Amanda came in with the kids, which wasn't part of the plan because I wanted to surprise them.

Jasmine walked over to me. "Mommy, he doesn't know when, but will you marry Daddy?" I heard what she said, but I had to repeat it in my head to make sure.

I looked at Bishop and realized that he didn't sit down but was down on one knee. "April, I'm going to make you a queen, and every-body is going to know our love is strong."

I felt a pull on my hand. "Mommy, you have to say yes, so I can give you this." Rose was standing there, holding a ring up to me.

"Of course I will marry your daddy. Yes, Bishop, I will marry you."

Rose handed me the ring, and Bishop grabbed me, so he could put it on my finger.

"Well, it looks like we're having a double wedding." I heard one of the twins say.

At first, I didn't get it, but then I remembered Blacky and looked over to see Lucky crying. They were in this together. I went over to hug her and said, "Look at us, two hood girls about to get married." There was so much joy in my heart as tears fell from my eyes. I hugged Bishop tightly before hugging my girls as well.

We were looking at our rings when Mama Kelly said, "Well, since April seemed to have forgotten what everybody was here for, I guess I'll say it."

I did forget, but I wasn't going to let anybody else give my surprise up. "Hold up. I got this, just let me get myself together." Standing in front of everybody, I said, "Bishop and Blacky ain't the only ones that can plan surprises. I have been ripping and running, trying to get this done. I hope that I picked right for everybody except Mama, Amanda, and Bull, who knew about this, so I told them to pick out their own gifts, but the rest of you, enjoy."

Amanda had the bags, but since the kids were there, I gave each one of them a bag and told them who to take them to.

The first thing they pulled out was a gas card, then there was a car title and key at the bottom.

"Girl, no, you didn't! You telling me I got a new car, and you held this from me?" Lucky asked.

"Lucky, I know you been having your eye on that Audi, and now you got it."

"Hell naw, this bitch done snapped! Who the hell you think you is, Oprah?" Kayla asked.

"If these kids weren't in here, I'll ask you something, but you and your bust-down sister must have laid it on them Mexicans because they dropped the money for all this plus some."

"Okay, enough of the talk. We got the keys; now, where do we get the car?"

I looked at Mama Kelly, and she nodded her head, so I said, "They're out front."

We all got up, but I waited until Bishop got up and followed him out. I was surprised he was still smiling, and he asked me, "What did you get yourself?"

I pointed at it when we got outside and said, "The Infinity."

"Bull must have told you that I liked the Hummer?"

"He said to get one of those Excursions, but since they stopped making them, I would have had to get you a slightly used one, so I got you the new Hummer instead," I replied.

"And they paid for all this?"

"In full. They wanted to get more expensive ones, but I knew you wouldn't like that, so with all the extra money, I got us a gas account with BP. Oh, and they hooked Bull and Nate up too. They have a whole line of cars, trucks, and limos for their business," I informed.

We sat back for a minute, watching everybody. The twins both got Lexuses, one red and the other white. I got Baby D a silver BMW, Blacky a Charger and a 300C, both all white. I wanted to get Corn a Porsche truck, but Mama Kelly talked me out of it, so I got him a dark blue Navigator and a black Escalade.

Corn stood by his Escalade and yelled, "Fuck y'all just standing there for? Let's spin some blocks and put some miles on these joints."

"Come on, baby. For once, let's go stunt on the hood," I spoke, looking up at Bishop.

"Well, let's take the dogs and the rest of the kids on a test drive and see how we look riding in these joints."

That was the calm before the storm. After that weekend and for the next six months, we seemed to be doing all the important stuff in shifts — spending time with the kids in shifts, sleeping in shifts, and somewhere in between that and business, we found a little time for each other.

CHAPTER SEVEN

Bishop

I WAS SITTING IN MY OFFICE, WORKING ON THE LAST OF THE PAPERWORK Kayla had taught me, so I could keep track of all the business I did for José and Jesus. Every two weeks, I gave Hectic my report for them, so they knew what I did for them — what I took for my chop and how much I owed them for what we got, which was mostly covered by what they paid me. I also had one for our payroll. It was an easy system, and I was able to keep track of all the money without having to go back to it and count it out like before.

Next to my work computer was my security monitor, and I looked at it when it started to beep, alerting me that somebody was at the front gate. Blacky's 300C was pulling into the gate with Corn in his Cadillac behind him. We got a shipment every two weeks, and while we tried to sit down once a week, the day after shipments were a must so we were all on the same page and everybody got their cut.

Kayla's desk set directly across from mine. There were three computers that sat on top of it, and she worked off every one of them. Our business was running smoothly, and that was something I was happy about.

I stood up from my chair. After sitting there for the last two hours, I stretched my arms over my head. "They got here early, so let's talk about the business end of things tomorrow, but as you know, I trust your judgment. I hope not to lose no money, but I'd rather have thirty thousand in dirty money or however you put that shit."

When Kayla was locked in on something, she didn't allow anything to distract her, and if she had to respond, she used few words. "Okay, cool."

She never stopped what she was doing, and I knew that was all I would get, so I shut everything down and moved the bags with Corn and Blacky's payroll money to the hallway. I went to the boardroom where they were already sitting, waiting on me. "What's good with y'all?"

Blacky was looking at his phone and just nodded at me.

"Bro came across some people tryin' to sell two apartment buildings and a house, and all they want is one point two. I told him to take the risk, at worse all three is a gut job, but the pictures look good, so I think it's a lick. He thinks he can get them to come down on the price, so his ass tryin' to prove it," Corn announced, pointing over to Blacky. "Who would sell two ten-unit apartment buildings in Wrigleyville, no matter the condition, and a four-bedroom four-bathroom house in Lombard for that price?"

Blacky looked up from his phone. "Somebody that's thirsty and needs the money now. Right now, they're not getting no play cause everybody thinkin' it's something wrong with the properties. But the only problem I see is the price, so to figure out what they really need, I cut the offer they made in half." Right then, his phone vibrated, and he turned his attention back to it.

April was busy making drinks, but when she brought them to the table, she looked at both me and Corn. "Bet the difference that he'll get it under a mil."

I never doubted him, so I turned to Corn to see if he'd take the bet; he shook his head no. Blacky finished texting. "They countered with $875,000, but they need at least half at signing. I told them they can get it all. Deal closed, nigga!" The last part was directed at Corn.

April started clapping. "I know that's right, Blacky. Show them they can't hustle a hustler."

I looked at Corn. "He should've stayed at half, but he know what he's doing, and it's well worth it."

Corn just waved his hand. "That nigga a used car salesman. He can sell water to a whale and buy hell from the devil."

We spent some time laughing and joking until I got back to business. "After we're done here, I'll be free, so if one of y'all need me to help elsewhere, let me know."

April was the only one to respond. "I could use some help at the row houses then. I'm going to teach Baby D and another one of the girls how to cook up. I'll be slowed up by that. If you can help, then I don't have to worry about catching up later."

"That's cool. How is everything else?"

"Good, the weed is moving good, and I'm pretty sure that we're keeping the blocks supplied, right, Blacky?"

Blacky nodded. "Yeah, we don't have no problems."

"Did you get to send that money to Looney?" I asked, looking over at April.

"I did that when I sent money to my people. I also sent a female to go visit him," she replied.

When I got out, I kept my promise to Looney. We sent him money every month and made sure his mom and child's mother were straight. The lawyer I had was able to get him a lesser charge, and he got twenty years at eighty-five percent, so he only had ten years left.

"I've been on the block workers about being on point. It's part of the game, but two niggas got robbed on our blocks, and it can't be a normal thing," Blacky informed.

"Did you holla at Bull?" I asked.

"I thought about it, but if these niggas give a fuck about their money, then they'll protect their shit like we did. Unless it becomes too bad and we start taking a loss, it's on them. It's at least a gun on each block, so if they stay on point, we won't need to go that far."

"Since everything is ready, I'm going to handle what I can tonight, then I need to go holla at that nigga, Cash, tomorrow about a few more spots I've been looking at. He wants a deal on the shit we sell him, but with that stunt he pulled with you, I'm only giving him what he got coming, and his ass lucky I'm not taxing him. The other change I'm making is I'm only going to sell heroin to this nigga over east. We're going to lose a little profit, but it's less people that we have to deal with, and since it's the hottest shit, I want niggas to think it's coming from somewhere else," Corn announced.

As soon as he mentioned Cash, I knew April was going to have something to say, and as soon as the last word came out of Corn's mouth, she got on it.

"Who is Cash, and what stunt did he pull with Bishop?" April asked, looking over at Corn.

Corn gave me the 'I fucked up' look, and I knew he wanted my help. "He's the nigga that got control over this area after Corn got locked up. Cash drove down on me one day, telling me to pay dues or shut down."

"Why didn't you tell me this before? It's like you fuckin' lied to me because you made it seem like you just didn't want to do it no more," April asked, anger evident in her tone.

"You're tripping, April. You know damn well I didn't lie to you. On them terms, I didn't want to do it no more."

"But you could've told me. You ain't say shit about the nigga pressin' you or nothing. Why would you keep that shit from me?"

"That's old shit. He should have told you, but at the same time, it was just y'all two, so it was for the best," Corn spoke, attempting to have my back.

Still, with a mug on her face, April said, "Okay, let's say fuck the past. How much is he charging us now, Corn?"

Corn didn't even look at her as he answered. "We give him three keys of coke each month."

"So, we give him seventy-five thousand for free and give him a play since he buys weight?" April asked, trying to comprehend what was being told to her.

"It sounds worse when you put it like that." Corn shook his head.

"Corn, you know it's bad, and he's trying to get a better deal. Fuck that, I'm going to talk to him tomorrow. Just tell me where and what time."

I had to jump in now. "You ain't going nowhere. That's Corn's job so let him handle it."

April looked at me, and there was fire in her eyes. "Last time I checked, I do have a say so, and I don't like the way that shit is going.

I think I can change it, so that's what I'm going to do," April said with so much anger in her voice that I knew had more to do with me going against it than her wanting to do it.

Corn cut in. "Homie, she got a point. You shut down because you weren't going for that shit. I'm not feeling it, and what about you, Blacky?" Blacky shook his head. "So, if we were to vote, feelings aside, it would be all four of us saying we don't go for that shit, and if she says that she wants to go fix it, then I say give her a chance."

Blacky cut in. "Yeah, I'm with Corn, and if need be, we can send somebody with her."

"Thank you, Blacky, but all I need is Miracle and Beauty, and that's only because I know it'll make Bishop feel better, but I can hold my own," April said.

They had a point, so I didn't try to argue. "If that nigga gets disrespectful, I'm personally going at that nigga."

"And we'll all be by your side, homie," Corn said.

"Is there anything else?" When nobody said anything, I stood up and said, "Well then, let's go do what we must. April, I'll be on Washington in like an hour." I took them to grab their money then told them that I'd catch up with them sometime tomorrow.

April came behind me as I closed the door. "Baby, you're not mad at me, are you?"

"On a business side, naw. Everybody agreed that something had to change the deal. And while I don't like it, I know you're capable of doing what needs to be done, so I can put my personal shit to the side. Now that shit you said about me lying to you did piss me off, but it's a dead issue so let's leave it alone."

"If you say so. Can I ride with you?" she asked.

"I'm not going straight there, and I might have to leave before you."

"That's cool, If you leave before me, I'll have Miracle bring me home."

"Well, let's ride then." I made it a daily thing to ride through all the blocks, and that was what I wanted to do before helping April.

"I got a question, Bishop. It's been close to a year, but Lil Tone's mom don't do shit. What's the plan with her?"

"Truthfully, I don't even know. I just don't want her out there like that," I replied.

"I can understand that, but everybody else is out here working for theirs and their family. She ain't shit, and while it's peanuts, she smokes for free, and she lives rent-free but don't do shit." I could tell April was tired of us helping her, so I knew something would have to shake.

"I will talk to her about that and come up with something, probably something like cleaning up the buildings and places we're working on."

"She a crackhead, so small shit like that shouldn't be nothing. But onto something else. We're going to do it after school is out, right?" April asked.

"That's the best time," I replied, already knowing what she was talking about.

She'd been dropping hints about the wedding a lot lately, and I knew she was thinking I was pushing it off, but I wasn't. I just had so much going on and didn't think now was the right time.

"I'm ready to start making plans. When is that going to happen?"

"I thought that you girls were going to handle that."

"Yeah, most of it, but we still need yours and Blacky's input."

"Okay, just tell us where to be and we'll be there. As long as it's for you and Lucky then we'll be happy."

"So, if I say everybody has to wear pink, then you would do it?" she joked, looking over at me, smiling.

"I'll wear the brightest pink you can find and probably look good in it too, but you would have to live with them damn pictures because we're only doing this once."

She hit me on the head then leaned over and gave me a kiss. "I was just testing you."

"You know I ride around every day, and it seems that all the blocks have a lot of niggas out there except the row houses," I spoke, changing the subject.

"I never paid it no mind, but I know money ain't slow over there."

"Yeah, it's still doing numbers, but a few times, it'll only be two niggas out there. It's all good in a way because security is always there to watch the house where everything is, but something got to be wrong."

"Ask Blacky. Better yet, ask whoever out there so you can see what's up and fix it if you need to," April said as we pulled up on the block.

I still couldn't get over the blue police lights flashing from the camera on the pole at the corner. As I parked, I thought that maybe that was the issue. Niggas were scared to hustle with the camera right there, especially since none of our other blocks had one.

I got out with April and waited until she went in the building where she had rented an apartment. I then focused on the alley and saw the one nigga that was always out there no matter what. He had a line of customers, so I just watched him do his thing. He couldn't be over sixteen years old. I looked around and saw three females in the alley selling weed, and that made me think of the times when I had to be out there every day.

As he finished up the line that he kept moving for a good two minutes, another guy walked up and took his place. I started to cross the street as he walked off.

"Aye, lil homie, let me holla at you." He stopped and waited on me as I jogged over to him. He was dressed for the cold night with a black Carhartt coat with the hood up, blue jeans, and wheat Timberland boots.

"What they call you?" I asked, wanting to know the guy's name.

He pulled his hood down, showing that he had neat dreads that went just past his ears, and he was almost the same tone as his boots. Seeing his face up close, I would put his age under sixteen. I wouldn't be surprised if his name was Babyface.

"Silk," he answered, looking me up and down.

"I'm Bishop. I see you out here damn near every day."

"Got to make some money, you feel me?" he told me.

"That's what's up, but where is everybody else? For a while now, it's only been a few of y'all out here."

"It used to be more, but since shit back to slamming everywhere, niggas started chasing money."

"You ain't making money out here?" I asked.

"It's good money out here, but you go to some other joints, and they make money plus whoever joint it is taking them shopping and other shit. So, compared to that, no," he replied.

"So, why you ain't follow this so-called money?"

"I did at first, but it's fool's money because you get paid less off a pack, so it's their money anyways, plus I really don't care about that shit. As long as I'm feeding my family and since ain't too many niggas over here, that's more money for me. Plus, these hoes that be selling weed stay ready to bust down, so I win both ways," Silk informed me, nodding his head.

"I'm a man about my family too, so I might not take you shopping, but if I can help you and your family then let me know."

"Unless my mom finds somebody to watch my baby sister and find a job then I got to do this. Shit, I'll probably still do it. I go two brothers that I never want to see involved in this, so I'll hustle to make sure they never have to."

"I can put your sister in daycare, and depending on what your mom wants to do, I can give her a job. Just give me her number and we can talk about it."

"If you can do that then maybe she'll finally feel comfortable enough to move out the hood, so you make that happen, then you'll have more than a hustler in me. I'll ride with you to the fullest," Silk replied, looking me directly in my eyes.

"Say no more. We gon' make that happen. Give me your number and I'll have the right people get up with you."

After he gave me the number, he pointed up the alley. "We stay right on West End. I can have her out here before you leave, and you can talk to her then."

"It'll probably be a few hours, but if I see you and it won't mess with the flow, we can do that," I agreed.

I let him get back to his hustle and walked back across the street to go help April. With new people being in this spot, I made note that we did need to secure this area better. What I really needed to do was figure out a way to make the owner sell two co-op buildings to me.

I laughed at myself when I realized that I didn't have a key to get in the building. I'd only been there with April, so I never needed one. Thankfully, it was the unit right at ground level, so I went to the front of the building and knocked on the window. I heard them laughing, and April yelled something before the door buzzed, and I heard the lock click.

I made sure to lock the apartment door and followed the sound of April's voice to the kitchen. She was standing at the kitchen table next to Baby D and a female so tall that I would expect to see her on a basketball court instead of learning to cook up crack. She was darker than me and had her hair braided straight to the back, dressed like a nigga. I knew she fucked with females, but she was here for business, so even if she was bad, that wouldn't matter.

Her and Baby D were focused as April measured everything on the table and put it in one of the four blenders on the counter. Each blender went for a minute, and April poured the content of each blender in its own mason jar. April had a system set up where she evenly measured out a quarter of a key, baking soda, and Remy. She had blenders with timers that were set for a minute. Anything more would fuck up the batch let April tell it.

She told them to grab one of the jars and grabbed the other two, and they walked to the stove and watched April put her jars in tall pots filled with salt water and followed suit.

April then turned to me. "Baby, this is Connie. She'll be working for us now. Connie, this is Bishop, my soon-to-be husband and always been my partner in crime."

I greeted her and Baby D then went to clean out the blenders they'd used. Another one of April's rules was to clean and start everything fresh after each batch. By the time we were finished cleaning, they were ready to start over, so I backed up and let them have the table and counter.

Knowing that April would have twice as much done in the time it was taking them to finish one key and not liking being a spectator, I grabbed a few keys and the rest of the supplies I needed before heading to the living room. I sat down and started mixing the cocaine and baking soda in the Ziploc bag, so they would only have to add the Remy blend and cook. When I heard the blender stop running, I would get up and clean up for them. After the third time, April finally noticed that I wasn't working in the kitchen.

She put her hand on her hip. "Boy, I thought you came over here to help me cook up not clean up then sit down twirling your thumbs."

I went to get everything that I had done and set it on the table. "I didn't wanna get in y'all way, so when you ready then all you gotta do is add the Remy, and it'll make up for the time you lost. If you want, we can all run a blender and pot on the stove."

"Now, that's genius. They got it; you know how good their teacher is. I'm gon' let 'em do their own thing one more time, then I'm gon' come help you." She turned to Baby D and Connie. "We gon' make shit easier for y'all, so y'all can take y'all time and get it right."

I stopped going back in the kitchen after that and focused on what I started. A while later, April came and sat across from me. I didn't know how long we worked, but we stopped at ten keys then put all the cooked-up work in big bags to take across the street to Lucky and Mona, so they could get it ready for the blocks.

When me and April took the work across the street to the bag up house, I saw that Silk was still out there. I didn't stop him from running the block, making us both money, but I did drive off feeling better that I knew the problem and how to fix it.

CHAPTER EIGHT

April

CASH. OF ALL NAMES, THAT WAS ONE OF THE LAST ONES I EXPECTED TO hear. I knew he'd got out, and I figured he still had his hands in the streets, but to find out he'd been running around, having people believe he was the man, then having the nerve to shut my baby down and take out of my mouth, his ass was lucky I didn't find out sooner because he wouldn't have shit coming if I did.

I knew if I told the boys we were going to cut Cash completely off, they wouldn't go for it, so I thought of ways to hurt his pockets without getting them involved, but the streets always talked, so I knew one way or the other, it would get back to them. I had to plan my moves just right, and when the time came, they would have no choice but to see things my way.

When Corn called to let me know where to be and the blocks that he wanted, he also told me he'd ride with whatever choice I made but not to do anything that made Bishop feel like he had to do something. We sometimes joked that he was too nice for the streets, but we knew if anybody fucked with our family, he'd show another side. Corn let me know we didn't need that right now, so with Miracle driving me in my Infinity SUV, I sat back and mentally prepare myself for the slick shit that I knew Cash was going to say.

We rode up on Cash's block, and the niggas were out there deep.

As we parked right in front of the two story, white house, it was clear that they had this spot going. Niggas were running up to cars to serve them, and more than a few were serving customers as they walked past. It was just like Cash to run a spot where he laid his head.

As Miracle parked, three niggas wearing hoodies and ski masks walked up and put their hand in their waistbands when they couldn't see through my tints. When me and Miracle got out, they pulled their masks off, exposing their faces, and instantly tried to holla at us. Even if I didn't have my man, I wouldn't have gave any of them a second look.

I went to the back door to let Beauty out, ignoring them. As I opened the door, one of them got up on me, and Beauty hopped out, and for the first time outside of training, I saw her ready to attack. She barked once and would've been on his ass if I didn't grab her.

The nigga jumped back with his hands up. "Damn, baby, get that thing."

"Nigga, I'm not your baby first off, and next time you come that close to me, it won't be good."

"My fault. I'm just trying to see what's up."

"That who I think it is?" I looked to where the voice came from and saw one of the best-looking men I knew standing on the porch. Dressed in a beige linen suit with a matching Chicago Bulls fitted cap was the one and only Cash. He looked just like my daddy from his chocolate skin to his tall, slim frame. I had to force myself not to get lost thinking of my daddy when I looked at his twin brother because while they looked and sounded the same, their personalities were as different as night and day.

"Princess, come give me a hug." I walked past all the niggas standing out there and opened the gate leading into the yard. When I stopped, not wanting to give the satisfaction to Cash by walking to him, Beauty sat down in the grass. Cash came down the stairs and pulled me in for a hug. He stepped back after a while and looked me over. "You looking good. Better than your moms and pops."

I put on my best fake smile. "Don't forget about uncle too."

I wanted him to think shit was all good until we were away from everybody.

"I don't know about all that, but I see you riding up all clean and shit. What that is?" he asked, pointing at my truck.

"Nothing but an Infinity."

"What, your pops bought it for you?"

"I send my parents money, so why would I need them to buy me a car? Me and my man work hard to have the best."

"Okay, Princess, I see you all grown up now and doing your own thing. Anyways, I'm waiting on somebody but come in the house. We have some catching up to do."

I turned to Miracle and said, "Stay out here while I handle this." I followed Cash into his house. As soon as we walked in the door, we were in the living room. I didn't have to ask Cash if he lived here because I already knew he did. The house looked like a trap house but was unfinished and dirty. However, I knew if I walked through the house, I would find his bedroom.

The living room had three long couches covered in sheets that did nothing to make me want to sit on it, but knowing that I would be there for a while, I took a seat. Even though she knew not to do it at home, I patted the seat next to me, and Beauty jumped up and laid her head in my lap. Cash sat on the couch across from me and picked up a blunt out of the ashtray on the table that was between us. It was littered with dirty plates and a stack of red cups and a bottle of some shit I'd never seen.

He held the unlit blunt my way. "You smoke, Princess?" I shook my head, not knowing what was in it. He pointed to the bottle of liquor. "What about drink?"

"I'm good, but I see you got this spot running real nice. You trying to follow in my daddy's footsteps?" Behind his head, I could see the rest of the house was just as dirty as the living room like I thought it would be.

"I'm not trying to get locked up, but I'm working on finishing what he started."

"Speaking of that, how long it's been since you got out?" I knew the answer already, but I wanted to hear it out of his mouth.

"I only did a year before they let me go. They didn't have proof that I was involved in anything," he replied.

"So, that's…" I counted in my head. "Twelve years ago, right?"

"Almost thirteen."

"So, twelve-plus years and this the first time I saw you or even heard from you? And I'm guessing my pops don't know what you're doing because he calls, writes, and I go visit him, but he didn't tell me nothing about you taking over," I spoke.

He took a hit from his blunt and smiled. "It's not like that, Princess. There's a lot of stuff that you don't understand," he said before blowing out the smoke.

"Okay then, tell me what it's like and I'll tell you what it is. I know way more than you think."

"I'll sit down with you later, but I have somebody coming over to handle some business, so I can explain when I got time after that."

"The person you're waiting on isn't coming. He sent me."

"Who sent you?" I saw the confusion on his face.

"Corn," I replied.

"That's who you call your man?"

"No, but I do believe you met my man before. You remember Bishop? That's my man, and you shut us down when I was pregnant."

"You mean the lil nigga that works for Corn? And you got a kid? Why didn't you bring the baby?"

"I got three kids, and my man don't work for nobody. We got a team, and he's the head of it." I knew I shouldn't have put our business out there, but I wanted to rub it in his face.

"I should've known. So many people have come saying your mom's work was back in the streets but better, and who would be able to do that but you?"

"Okay, Uncle Cash, now that we're all caught up, can you explain why all these years went past and not once did you come looking for me? Why in all these years doing whatever it is that you're doing not once did you send your own brother some money after he did whatever it took to get you out? Even though you're really the one that fucked up and why everybody went down?"

He balled his face up and sat back on the couch. "That's what he told you?"

"If it's one thing I don't like about my dad, it's that he won't speak a bad word about you, even when he knows you're wrong. But I was old enough to recognize that stuff was going wrong. I could see the shit myself. Plus, my mom didn't have a problem telling me that you were the cause of their downfall."

"Look, Princess, I'll be the first to admit I made a mistake. Shit, probably more than a few but what could I have done for you? I got out and had to lay low just in case they were watching me."

"That's bullshit, Cash, because you were collecting dues off all the blocks, so if you were getting twelve thousand from us, you had to be getting at least twenty or thirty times that each month." I looked him in his eye, letting him know I knew about everything.

"I had to pay niggas to make sure that shit went smooth."

"So, you couldn't find a few thousand for your brother, or you couldn't come get me out a stranger's house where anything could've happened? You had so much on your plate that nobody else even mattered, but you had time to ride down on niggas that was on their hustle and take out of their mouths?" I was starting to get mad, but I wasn't going to let it show because I was more determined to get even.

"If I would've known he was your lil boyfriend, I wouldn't have did him like that," Cash admitted.

"That's not even the point. Why do anybody like that? Go make your own money."

"Your pops did it. So, what's wrong with me doing the same thing?" he asked, this time looking me in my eyes.

"Don't lie on him. He sold to them several times to put some of his work out there to pay for the block."

He didn't have anything to say once he saw I knew what I was talking about. I wanted to see how he would respond to what I had planned for him.

"Now, how would you feel if Bishop came and shut you down?"

"Don't be silly now, Princess. We both know that shit can't happen."

"You may think it's silly, but what if we stop selling you weight? Then what? How you gonna make money then?"

"I'll still get dues from a bunch of the blocks out west, including most of the blocks that y'all got. Princess, I've been in the game way too long to let a nigga that's still wet behind the ears beat me."

"But that's the thing. He's barely been in it, and he's your connect. Plus, he got some people on his team that if he give the word, they would walk all over you, so if he has to show you who has the most power, do you think we'll pay you for our blocks?"

"April, no matter what you think, I love my family, and I'll never take it there with you or this boy, especially since it seems like he's taking good care of you. If we can move on with you giving me a chance to right my wrongs, then I'll do what I can."

I started listing the blocks that Corn wanted then said, "I want them, the ones we have, and when we're ready to expand, we want to get any block that we want. We'll keep selling you weight for twenty each for now, but we're done paying these monthly dues."

"Princess, all you had to do was call me, and I would've been did that. You didn't have to come over here trying to make me feel guilty," Cash said, throwing his hands in the air.

"I didn't know you were out here doing this until yesterday, and I wanted to do it face to face. That being done, I won't feel bad about what I have to do next."

He rubbed his hands over his face before he let out a sigh and said, "I don't know what that means, but you got what you asked for, and you said you'll want more in the future. I can do that, but what else do you feel you need to do? If it's reasonable, whatever you ask for will be done."

"That's the thing, Cash. I shouldn't have to ask for what I want, so when the time is right, I'm just going to take what belongs to me. And you better believe that you'll know about it, but till then, you better make the best of this time because it won't last long."

When I finished talking, I got up and just walked out, so he couldn't respond. Knowing him, he probably had a stupid look on his face, which would've been priceless if I would have turned around. However, I didn't want him to see the anger on my face, so I kept walking out the door.

Miracle was already in the car with it running, and as soon as I got in with Beauty, she drove off. I waited until we got a block away before pulling out my phone to call Bishop, but Miracle put her hand on my arm to stop me.

"Give yourself some time to cool off. You look mad as hell right now, and I'm sure you'll sound like it too. The last thing we need is for your people — or my brother — thinking dude did some crazy shit."

I put my phone in my lap, taking her advice since I knew that was what they'd think, and while I wouldn't mind somebody putting a bullet in Cash's face, I did what I set out to do for now.

After driving around a little more, Miracle pulled over and turned toward me. "He didn't get crazy, did he?"

I shook my head. "It just was more emotionally taxing than I thought it'd be." I took a deep breath. "I'm telling you since you'll be with me, but I need you to keep this between us for now." I looked at her to look in her eyes. "Deal?"

She gave me a hesitant nod. "As long as it don't have to do with your safety."

"Cash, the man I just went to see, is my daddy's brother. Nobody knows that."

"So, he's your uncle?" She gave me a confused look as she asked me.

"My daddy's brother. I will not claim him as any kind of family anymore. He's the reason my family got split up. While my parents are doing a bunch of time, he has his freedom. Today was the first time I saw him, and as you see, it had me feeling some type of way," I revealed.

"Yeah, that explains a lot. I don't know you that well, but it's part of my job to read body language, and you been going through it since I picked you up. For a second, I thought that was you dealing with the pregnant emotions."

I shook my head. "No! Don't wish that on me right now, girl. The last thing we need is another baby. But you're right. I've been going through it since I heard his name."

Acting like a sister, Miracle reached over and rubbed my hand. "Make your call and tell me where we're going."

I did feel a bit calmer, so I called Bishop. When he picked up, I asked, "Where you at, baby?"

There was a lot of noise in the background, and it was hard to hear when he answered. "I'm at one of the houses that we're fixing up. Why? You good?"

"I know you want to know what happened, but if you're busy, then I'll tell you later."

"Me and Corn is over here on Gladys and Central. Come through the alley and you'll see us," Bishop replied.

I told him I'd be there in a few minutes. Right before I ended the call, he spoke. "I took care of that with Mama T too. I really think she was happy, and if you see her, she looks a lot better."

"Good for her. I'll see you in a bit."

As we pulled up, we saw Blacky's Charger and followed him to the house they were fixing. When I got out the car, the noise from all the machines and hammering made hearing anything almost impossible. I had to cover my nose, so I wouldn't breathe in the sawdust hanging in the air. As I got closer to Bishop, I heard him yelling out instructions to the people they had working for them. Corn came out the back of the house, and we all went and sat in Blacky's car to block out the noise. Bishop got in the back with me, and they all turned to me, wanting to know what happened.

"Well, we had a lil talk, and in the end, I agreed that we would keep giving him the low price like everybody else that cops from us, but we're not paying to put work on blocks. We get all the blocks that Corn wanted now plus any we want in the future."

"And he didn't have a problem with that?" Corn asked, looking surprised.

"He was more than happy to agree, and if there is anything else, he'll do it," I replied.

"As long as he was respectful and something came out of it, then I'm good." Bishop shrugged.

Blacky spoke up. "I don't know buddy, but y'all make it seem like he's one of those super grimy niggas that only give a fuck about self. This don't sit right with me. He gotta be on something else. He can't be the grimy ass nigga y'all say then just agree to something like that without pushback."

"As long as he doesn't bring it this way, fuck him. But on another note, I know you're familiar with most of the workers, Blacky, so I need you to find some of the laidback ones and see if they'll go over on Washington," Bishop spoke.

"I know a few that could fit in," he answered.

"Good and April, if you got some extra time, can you go on Washington? It's a nigga out there named Silk. Can you take his mom to go talk to Nate about a job? Then, take her to the daycare, so she can see where her daughter will be, and holla at Mama Kelly about renting one of the houses."

"That's all?" I asked.

"Call Blacky when you drop her off, so he can get her a car."

I agreed, and since all of them were staying there, I hugged them saying, "Love y'all."

CHAPTER NINE

Bishop

TIME HAD BEEN FLYING, AND THE ONLY WAY I WAS ABLE TO KEEP track of it was when I had to meet up with Hectic. Even though we had to take care of business, he made time for me to get shit off my chest. Most of the time, it was me talking the problem out with myself, but today, it wasn't. Hectic and I were due to have one of our monthly games of chess. I enjoyed this time because it was the one time we put business to the side and just relaxed.

Today, as we sat across from each other in a hotel room, battling it out in a chess game, the conversation turned to something that I didn't have a plan or solution for.

Hectic sat back and clapped his hands once. "Tomorrow is the big wedding day, huh?"

I didn't take my eyes off the board, focusing on my next move. "Yeah, it's finally here."

"You nervous?" When I didn't answer, he kept going. "I hear that being a married man is hard work."

"Damn, Hectic, I thought you was on my side. Wait till I tell April that you're trying to talk me out of it."

"Don't do that! I just got to make sure you know what you're doing," he confessed.

"I think she would've been happy without it, but we've been

together for almost twelve years. I love her, and I know she loves me. Ain't none of that gon' ever change."

"You got a good one." He made his move on the chess board. "Do you like the gift from José and Jesus?"

"A week in Jamaica? Hell yeah!" They let me know as soon as we set a date, so I wouldn't plan a honeymoon.

"How about another week in Puerto Rico?"

"Shit, how about it?" I made my move.

He studied the board and then asked me, "Why would you do that? If I take that, you won't get nothing in return."

"If I move anywhere else, then I'll be playing to get a stalemate. I want to win or lose trying to win." I watched as he took my rook, which left room for me to make my other moves. After the third move, he stared at me, finally seeing the setup. *Checkmate.*

"Play to win or lose trying to win; I like that. Is that the way you look at things, hustler?" Hectic asked, smiling at me.

"That's the way it is. You said it yourself that your mindset determines your outcome, so I got my mind set on winning, and nothing else is even acceptable."

"How much more winning do you need to do? You have been winning in everything you do."

"Yeah, because in my mind, losing isn't an option, and as long as I keep that in mind before every move, I'm bound to win no matter what I'm doing. If I'm not winning in one thing, I want to be winning in the next thing I set out to do."

"Well, before you make the next move, enjoy tonight. I'll see you tomorrow and have some fun in Puerto Rico. I don't think one week is enough, so this is my gift to both of you couples," Hectic stated.

"I'm not going to argue, good looking."

"I already talked to Corn, and he said that he can handle all the business, so don't worry about that either."

"MAN, you niggas looking fly as fuck. Kind of makes me want to get married," Corn said as we stood at the door.

"Corn, your ass got to settle down with somebody first," I said as I fixed my bowtie.

"Oh, yeah, I forgot about that part," Corn joked.

All the guys stayed at Corn's house for the night, and the ladies stayed at ours with April. Now, we were waiting on the limo.

Corn looked at Blacky and said, "What's up, homie? You been extra quiet all morning. Look at him. That nigga scared."

When he grunted, I knew it was true because I was feeling the same way too. I put my hand on his shoulder. "Homie, this the easy part. We just got to find a way to keep them happy enough for the rest of our lives, and if all else fails, just get her pregnant." We all laughed.

"Easy for you to joke about but y'all just don't know that Lucky planned this wedding around the time of her ovulation. She got set times we're going to fuck, nothing less than twice a day, and now you tell me that we're going to be gone for two weeks."

Corn sucked his teeth. "This nigga complaining about getting too much pussy while I'm going to be here hoping that I can find time to fuck." I shook my head.

"Let's go, rides are here," Bull stuck his head through the front door to say.

"Real talk, Bull, it's your day off," I said. "Whoever you hired to do security, that's their job. You just be my homie."

"It'll be hard, but I got you," Bull agreed.

When we stepped outside on the way to the limo, I looked at the sky and took a breath and felt the sun on my face. "Damn, if we would've known it was going to be this nice, I would've had the wedding outside."

"Please don't say that around Lucky. She wanted that so bad, and it's the perfect day for it. The sun is out, not too hot, and they say it's going to be like this all day. I might not hear the end of it." Blacky shook his head.

I threw my arm around his shoulder as we walked the rest of the way to the limo. "Let's take it as a sign that it's going to be a good day. An even better start to us being married men."

We had a limo for the guys because we wanted to ride together. The girls had one for April and Lucky, two for the bridesmaids, and another for the kids, Amanda, and Mama Kelly. Blacky had his family and Lucky's family staying at his house, so there was another two limos for them. Plus, Bull had I didn't know how many more cars just so we wouldn't get split up, but I really thought it was his way of adding security.

We didn't want it to be in a church, so the whole thing was going to be at a hotel. It was a thirty-minute drive, and Blacky kicked it off by drinking because the limo had a bar, then everybody, including Silk, took a shot.

We arrived at the venue first and were sure to be inside the hotel before April and Lucky even pulled up. I was told it was because it was bad luck to see the brides before the wedding. We invited about seventy-five people, mostly people that we had a business relationship with. We tried to keep it on the legal side, but there were a few we sold to and loyal workers like Silk and his family that we felt comfortable letting come.

Both Blacky's and Lucky's parents stayed out of state, so this was the first time we'd met either of them. We were able to meet a lot of Blacky's other family as well. All of them came from out of town.

Me, Blacky, Bull, and Silk went to the altar while Corn waited for April since he was going to walk her down the aisle. We were told where to stand since Bull was both of our best man. He stood in the middle of us, and the preacher was a step above him. When everybody that came with us was seated, *The Wedding Song* by Jamie Foxx played. It was the same song he sang on his show when he got married.

The door on Blacky's side opened, and Lil Man came walking out, then Jasmine walked out throwing flowers, followed by Lucky and her dad. Once she was next to Blacky, the other door opened, and Lil John came walking to me, followed by Rose with the flowers. It was only a few seconds, but it seemed like minutes before April was in the doorway.

I knew that Corn was with her, but our eyes locked on each other as it seemed like she was gliding toward me.

With her in front of me, the preacher started. We listened to Blacky and Lucky say their vows and exchange rings. However, as I was turning back toward April, a movement in the back caught my eye. At first, I didn't think anything of it, but then, I recognized the face. I knew he wasn't invited, so what the fuck was he doing here?

APRIL

EVERYBODY THAT KNEW Bishop could tell that something was wrong, and when I followed his eyes, my stomach dropped. When I saw who it was, I knew something was going to happen. My eyes shot to Bull since I knew he'd be the first to move, but none of his people would do anything without his word. I looked out and saw Miracle looking at me; she knew it wasn't a threat. When I shook my head, she sent a sign to Bull, who looked at me with a confused look on his face. Knowing I had to get things back on track, I grabbed Bishop's hand, so he would focus on me. When he looked at me, I said my vows to him.

"Bishop, I told you I didn't want you to put a speech together because the day that you asked me to be your wife, you said enough. Any more words would ruin all the surprises that you could bring into my life, so I ask only that you keep being the man that you are. I won't call it love at first sight, but you came in my life during my darkest days and shined some light on me, and since then, you've made me fall in love with you over and over again. You have given me three beautiful children of my own and two more that are like mine. I now have brothers and sisters, another mom, and everything that a family should be. Bishop, you have given me all that I ever wanted, and to show you just how much you mean to me and the amount of love that I have for you, I turn my life over to you. I have shown you that I can be a down ass bitch and the best mother possible, but now, I'm going to show you the wife I can be and take my place as the queen next to my king."

It got quiet for a few seconds, then everybody started clapping when they realized that I was done. It took a while for it all to die down, but finally, we were able to exchange rings, and Bishop kissed me for the first time as his wife.

When all the formalities were out of the way, the staff from the hotel started moving the chairs to give us room to dance. There was a

DJ playing music, and everyone was doing a two-step, but I still had one worry.

I knew shit was going to turn ugly if I let Bishop and my uncle get close to each other, so I tried to stay close to Bishop. However, with everybody trying to congratulate me and see the rings that me and Lucky got, I ended up losing track of him until Miracle tapped me and pointed to all the guys gathered up. It was a sign that let me know that they were up to something, so I started to make my way toward them, but Cash took that moment to walk in the door with his guys right next to where Bishop was standing.

I got close enough to hear Bishop say, "I don't know what you're doing here, but I'm giving you one chance to leave before this turns ugly."

Cash threw both of his hands up. "I'm not looking for trouble; that's not why I'm here."

Bull stepped forward. "Then leave before you get it. This is a private ceremony."

Cash gave that smile that was his way of being slick. "But I was told to come give my niece away."

"Well, you ain't got no niece or family here, so whoever invited you fucked up." Bishop never got loud, and I could tell that he was getting to that.

I stepped between Bishop and Cash, holding my hands out between the both of them. "What the fuck is you doing here? You don't just pop up at my wedding and think it's all good," I spoke, looking over at Cash. I could feel my anger boiling, but I was not going to allow him to ruin my day.

"I didn't just pop up. Dolla sent me his invite and told me to come on his behalf and walk you down the aisle."

"April, what the fuck is going on? This nigga talking like he really knows you. And who the fuck is Dolla? And why the fuck is he sendin' niggas to walk you down the aisle?" Bishop asked, looking over at me.

I knew the truth was going to get out, but I didn't want it like this, and I wasn't about to let it mess up my wedding day.

I turned to Bishop. "I know there's going to be some explaining to do, but we agreed to put all business to the side till after our honeymoon, so we'll put everything on the table then. For now, I'll tell you that Cash is my pops' brother." I grabbed Bishop's hands.

"So, he's your uncle?"

"Not in my eyes but can we please talk about it later?" I asked with pleading eyes.

He only nodded his head, which was a bad sign since he didn't talk when he was mad or was planning something.

Once Cash left, everything went back to normal. We had our first dance, and Bishop surprised me by knowing how to move. We cut our cake, and even though he promised not to, Bishop smashed cake in my face, but to see him laugh and smile was all worth it. I knew then our lives together would be wonderful.

CHAPTER TEN

Bishop

DAMN, I COULD GET USED TO THIS. OUR HONEYMOON WAS THE definition of living. The first thing we saw was the sunrise as we landed in Jamaica. The beaches made the setting relaxing, unlike the city, and we did things we never even thought of doing. What nigga from the hood had been hang gliding, snorkeling, or just laid out on white sand beaches? We went on rides around both islands and took a helicopter ride over Puerto Rico? I knew we had some good weed, but the shit the Jamaicans had was on a whole other level. We were told we had to try it, and when we did, it was like it gave us that heavenly feeling. April just wanted to go back to the room and fuck. I knew we were going to make a baby for sure after that.

The streets were the farthest thing from my mind, and not only did I look forward to all the things that me and April would do together in life with our family, but it was a time to reflect and get our minds right before we got back and faced life. I just wished that I could have done this with my mama and even Lil Tone because this was the life that I wanted to have with them.

When we got back home, my mind went right back to business, and I wanted to address the issue about Cash, but when we saw the kids, I knew I had to give them my time. It had been weeks since we saw them, and I missed my babies like crazy.

I wanted to make sure my kids got to have a childhood, so I had Amanda plan out the rest of the summer for our kids and Blacky's, so there was something for them to do every day. It felt like we were all doing things for the first time together. I had never been to a zoo. So, when we went to the Brookfield's Zoo, all the kids were teaching me about the animals. We had so much fun at the water park, Magic Waters, in Rockford that other kids wanted to come play with us the whole day. The best time we had, however, was some shit that only Amanda would have thought of; we spent a weekend camping outside. I knew our kids would have more memories than we did as kids.

I waited till the first meeting that we had to bring up the Cash situation. I let all the normal business get handled before I got to it.

"So, of course, April knew about her uncle, but I want to know if anybody else knew," I said while looking at Blacky and Corn.

Blacky spoke first. "Everybody knows who Dolla and Cash is; I don't give a fuck where you from in the city. Now, if I would've known that Dolla was her dad, of course I would've known that Cash was her uncle, but I found all that out at the same time as you. My hands is clean on this one, and really, I think this is more on the personal side."

I turned to Corn cause, in my mind, he knew this whole time and just held it back from me, and I wanted to know why.

Corn took a sip of water. "Look, homie, I got the vibe that you think that because I'm out in the streets that I knew something, but on some real shit, I slipped on that. Now, after y'all left, I did get the whole story, and if April don't mind, I want to tell the part that has something to do with my moms and pops."

"April don't got no say in what can be said till I say so."

"Come on, bro. You're tripping saying it like that. Maybe she did fuck up, but when we at this table, we're going to talk to each other with the love we hold for each other." I knew Corn was right, and my words came off wrong, but I'd held this shit in too long, and I wanted to know what was what.

"Clearly, you know more than I do, so I'll wait to say my peace." April looked at me as she said that, even though she was talking to Corn. She looked mad as hell, but I didn't care at the moment.

"So, to be clear, I didn't know that Dolla was her pops and Cash her uncle. Nobody knew what happened to Princess after the Feds took everybody in, and the only person in Chicago that knew April was back was my moms," Corn said.

"Wait, how did Mama Kelly know me?" April asked, and I was wondering the same thing.

"I really wish she would come to tell the story herself, but she says it's not her business. So, to break it down the best way I can, and trust me I just found this out, but my pops' name was Top Hat. He was Dolla's righthand. Dolla's name is Top Dolla; my moms was super tight with the queen herself. She was older, so she gave April's mom the game of being a hustler and gangster's wife. This was before April was born, and I was younger. They ended up finding my pops in the trunk of his car, shot up. Now, this story might sound familiar to y'all, but nobody can say for sure. They think that Cash had something to do with it because he was tired of playing second to my dad in Dolla's world."

"So, if nobody could prove it, then why did they think Cash did it?" I asked.

This was going farther back than I thought, but I wanted to know who I was dealing with. "Mainly because nobody else would have caught him slipping like that. He had a rule that nobody in the inner circle could be in the streets alone, so they won't get done like that or nobody could work with the Feds. That night he went missing, the only person that wasn't with somebody else was Cash, so there was only whispers, but nobody would say it out loud because Top Dolla would've killed them. Everybody knows Top Dolla's weakness, and that's Cash. My moms said that if it was anybody else, their whole bloodline would have been wiped out. All he ever said was they were looking for who did it, and by the time April was born, it wasn't talked about no more. That's when my moms walked away, but she stayed in touch with the queen, and that's how she recognized April, but when April didn't mention her uncle, she figured it was a smart move, her words not mine."

"So, if you don't mind, Bishop, I'd like to talk now," April said with some attitude in her voice.

"Yeah, explain why I had to find this out like I did."

"Okay, first thing, that's not my uncle. To me, he's my dad's brother and nothing more. It's a lot to it, but on some simple shit, I know he's the person that got my parents popped by the Feds. His ass is so selfish that he didn't send nobody a dime when he got out, so after hearing how he did you, I decided to keep my personal feelings out of it and focus on business concerning him."

"So, what you saying is that you don't want to fuck with your own blood?" I asked, wanting to be clear about what she was saying.

"Right now, I have to, and since we're married now, I'm supposed to be queen of the city and you the king. After we go visit Daddy, we take over, and we don't have to deal with him no more."

I said nothing for a while. What she was saying made sense, but there was no reason for her to keep it from me before, so I had to make sure of one thing first.

"Corn, do you have a problem with this nigga?" I asked, looking over to him.

"Real shit, I don't know what to think. I've been so caught up running our shit, I kind of put it to the back of my mind. Right now, I'm focused on business. The only way that would change is if my moms tells me more or if it gets crazy."

"April, I think I know how you feel but go ahead and tell me."

She looked at me and said, "I don't like him, and when Daddy lets me have the title that he promised me, then I will make him the lowlife he is. I won't make the same mistake and let him take us down."

I wasn't sure if she was done, so I waited before turning to Blacky. "What's your thoughts?"

"I don't think none of us like his ass. It's more personal with y'all, so I say if we can cut him off without no bullshit, then we do that." He shrugged.

"I'm not worried about no bullshit. That can be handled real quick, but he's still part of April's family, even if she doesn't claim him. I bet Dolla does, so I'm not making my vote till I see him next week. We can get back up when we get back and take it from there."

I told Corn the last bit that we all agreed to without him. "Homie, you held it down while me and Blacky were being used as slaves, also known as our honeymoon, so pick a spot and go live it up for a week. I would give you two weeks, but you need to get married for that."

"And we know that's not about to happen," April spoke.

"Shit, that nigga can have two weeks if he has a girl for over six months," Blacky said.

"Ha, ha, y'all got jokes, but I'm most definitely taking that week."

"Hold up, I need you to take Silk and his girl with you. I want homie to see more than the streets, and you said he helped hold shit down," I informed.

"Yeah, I doubt homie slept. That's how much he was out there."

"So, do that and send me the bill. It's on me."

"Oh, then you best believe your pockets about to get lighter."

We all laughed and got up to leave. April caught me before I went to the money room.

"So, you mad at me?"

I looked at her and thought about what she could do to make me mad at her, and the few things were shit I knew she wouldn't do.

"Look, I tweaked by talking to you like that, but you know that none of this even matters without our family. So, I'm not letting nothing that happens in that room come into our family life."

"I love you, soon-to-be king of Chicago."

"I love you too, queen of my family."

CHAPTER ELEVEN

Bishop

WE KNEW THAT IT HAD TO BE DONE, ESPECIALLY AFTER THE SHOWDOWN at the wedding with Cash. As soon as Corn got back, me and April decided to fly down and visit her dad.

We had just pulled up outside of USP Beaumont in Texas where Dolla was locked up at. I parked and turned to April. "I can't lie to you. I'm nervous as hell. I wish that we did this before all the bullshit with Cash. Now, it feel like me and him both got a first impression without even meeting."

April leaned over and kissed me. "I wish I can tell you not to be, but I probably feel worse. Not only do I hate seeing him like this, but I could've made this first meeting better for y'all. Trust me though. Daddy will make it easy on us."

"Well, it's not going to get any easier just sitting here." We got out and went through the long ass process to sign in. I wasn't just nervous about meeting Dolla. It was this thing about putting myself in a prison after them people tried to make me spend the rest of my life in one.

When we were finally escorted to the visiting room with a group of other people, mainly women and children, I was surprised to be in a public visitation area filled with visitors. I thought that it would be like the visiting room in the county jail, and we'd be separated by a glass. As we sat down at a table for four, I looked around at all the niggas locked up and knew that I could've been in the same position. Seeing most of them laughing and smiling with their people, I turned to April sitting to the left of me. "Shorty, you think these niggas really happy?"

She looked around to see what I was talking about. "I don't know. You was locked up, and when I came to visit you, you was smiling. Was you happy?"

I didn't need to think about that. "Hell naw. Maybe for that moment but even then, I still knew that you'd be leaving, and I'd be stuck there. I don't think they could be happy here, but they look it."

"Yeah, baby, you smiled, but I could tell you wasn't happy, and I bet their people can see through the mask, but if they're here, then they know the things that's small but will bring a smile or 'happy moment' as you put it," April spoke.

I shook my head because that was the truth. "I guess besides freedom, that's all they can ask for."

We sat there for another minute before I saw her dad walking toward us. April jumped up and damn near ran to give him a hug. I was stuck because even if somebody were to bet me everything that belonged to me, I would bet it that this was the same nigga that popped up at my wedding.

April snapped her fingers. "Bishop, get up and meet my daddy." I got up and went around the table to shake his hand. "And Daddy, meet my husband, Bishop."

We sat down, Dolla sitting across from me, putting me in the mindset that we were about to play a game of chess.

He started laughing and said exactly what I was thinking. "Yeah, me and my brother look just alike, don't we?"

I didn't understand why he was saying that with pride, but I answered. "If I didn't know better, I would say y'all was the same nigga. Y'all identical for real."

"I wish we was, but my twin seems to rub most people the wrong way. I just didn't know that you had a bad encounter with him in the past. I would've never sent him to represent me at y'all wedding. I don't do it often, but you deserve my apologies."

"I understand, but I'm not going to hold you accountable for his actions."

"That'll be the first." Even though April said it under her breath, we both heard her. When he didn't say anything about it, I moved on too.

"Even though you missed being there in person, I hope all of the pictures made you feel like you had front row seats. That was the motto of the company we hired to do the pictures."

I knew that I was just nervous talking, so when he just nodded to what I said, I didn't say anything else.

Finally, after a minute, he started talking. "Bishop, I've been asking around bout you, and I don't know what to take from what I hear. On the street level, nobody seems to know where you stand. I got some people questioning if you're even in the game because we can't find nobody you cop from."

I didn't hear any questions, so I stayed quiet, and he kept going. "But I know better than that, so I asked who you messed with, and they say Top Hat's boy, who's moving weight like he makes it, so I went a step higher and asked about him, and nobody in that circle knew him. Now, imagine my surprise that when I said Bishop, the very next name they said was April, my Princess. I find it hard to believe, but they say that not only are you liked but respected by people that neither like nor respect Blacks."

I recognized that my best move was to listen and his worse was to talk, which he kept doing. "Then, what really messed my head up was them telling me about how a few cartels banded together just because of the team that you and April put together. No disrespect but at first glance, I don't see the person they describe."

I wanted to laugh because that was either a joke or a test. I took it as a joke but responded like a test. "I guess none taken, but at first glance, what am I supposed to look like?"

Dolla leaned his head to the side and looked at me like that was going to tell him something. "I've been around many people of power, and you can just tell with them. I'd like to think that's the same way people see me before they know my name, and I don't get that from you."

I nodded, understanding what he was saying, though I still took it as a joke. I leaned in and held his eye contact. "That's because you're going off what somebody else has to say about me. I present myself as the person I see myself as, and I guess being a person of power ain't my strong suit."

"Okay, that makes sense. Then let me ask you. Who is Bishop?"

I wasn't about to come right out and tell my business, so I thought about all of the things I was besides a hustler, and that was what I told him.

"I'm a father of five, a husband, provider, brother, businessperson, and a man. That's who I am."

Dolla leaned back in his chair and stared at me for a few seconds before he started clapping, making people look our way.

"Now, that's what the fuck I'm talking about." He turned and looked at April. "Even though I wish I had met him beforehand, Princess, I approve. This might be the one man on Earth that will treat you better than I can."

April grabbed his hand. "Well, if you feel that way, Daddy, that means I can have my title, right?"

"What title do you want, Princess?"

"You told me that if I ever got married to a man that you approved of that I'll be the queen of Chicago." The look that she gave him reminded me of my baby girls when they wanted something from me. Now I knew all girls had that look for their daddy.

"Baby, you don't want that. It won't bring nothing but heat to y'all just like it did to me and your moms. I don't want that life for you. I'm sitting in prison now so that you wouldn't make the same mistakes that I made."

"No, your brother did that, but I don't have people like that around me. So, I can promise you I will never make those mistakes."

"That's your uncle. What is your problem with him anyways?"

April held up her hand and started making points on each finger. "The biggest is that he is the reason that you and my mother is locked up. Then, he was freed and never came for me. When we were out there hustling for our money, he shut us down for not paying block fees. He's been charging everybody in the land fees, saying that's what you did. And through it all, I bet he still ain't send you a dime. Do I need to say more?"

"Okay, he ain't perfect, but he's still family, so you can't just cut him off. He needs to eat too."

"For you, Daddy, I'll give him a hundred thousand to stay out the way." She smiled, knowing she was trying him.

"That's crumbs, and you know it, but he won't step back so include him in your plan, and you can have what you want."

I was sitting back, thinking of a way to say what was on my mind, but I didn't know how to say it any other way.

"When I say this, Dolla, don't take it as disrespect, but we run them streets. I might not be the full-on gangsta type, but I got niggas that is, and anything we want, we can get it. I can't take this title that she wants since it can only come from you for it to mean something to her, so tell me what it'll take."

"Keep my brother in play."

"She doesn't want that," I replied.

"You the man."

"But she's my woman. I respect her feelings and her input," I stated.

"She's working off emotions."

"And you're moving off blind loyalty."

He paused, and to me, that was like saying check, and while I wasn't trying to mate him, I had to keep pushing him back, so he'd see things my way.

"Look, I know she won't like it, but I'm big on family, so I understand. Same time, I have a bigger family to protect, and nothing will mess that up. So, Cash won't be anywhere near us. We will come up with a reasonable deal where he'll get more than he deserves and enough space to move it. In exchange, he'll stay out our way, leave our blocks alone, and of course, my wife gets her title."

I knew that he saw no way out and was stalling to see if I would add something, but it was his move next. After a few minutes, he asked, "So, how this deal going to look?"

"I can't say for sure because our team will have to agree. I'm thinking a few keys a month should be enough, but my deal won't change, so you need to tell him to take it and keep his end of it."

"Consider it done and good luck on being the new king and queen of Chicago. If I say so myself, both of y'all got some big shoes to fill."

I thought that April was going to be jumping for joy, but all she did was smile and say, "Thank you, Daddy. We won't let you down."

I listened to them talk about the old days before Dolla had gotten locked up. April was all smiles, and I knew a visit with her daddy was exactly what she needed. The only time I spoke was to ensure what I would send would be exactly what he wanted.

When we got back in the car, I asked April, "Is everything good now?"

"More than good. I was surprised that you had Daddy stuck, and I hate that we have to give his brother a crumb, but you got me what I wanted, so I'm happy."

"That's good, but I don't understand how you can look at your uncle and hate him when he looks just like your dad."

"They used to be the same to me. When I was a little girl, you couldn't tell me shit. I had two daddies, but when I got older, I saw Cash for who he was. Only me and my mom could tell them apart. It's all in the eyes. That's what I hate in Cash and love in Daddy."

Driving out the parking lot, I considered it a blessing that the visit turned out just as planned because April got what she wanted. The only thing that I let slide was his comment about filling some shoes. The ones I wore fit just right as long as my family was taken care of.

April

I KNEW Bishop would stay true to his word that he gave Daddy, and while I didn't want to give Cash shit, I was okay with something, just not what they came up with. I was mad as hell, but I knew how to play on Cash's pride, so when he did or said something stupid, Bishop would go off.

I thought of a way to really get under Cash's skin. I told Bishop to show him that we really had the power, we needed to show up on Cash's block deep as hell and without calling first. What Bull set up made it seem like the president was about to slide through. When we got there, our guys jumped out and had the whole block on lock.

Miracle opened my door, and Bull let Bishop out. I knew Cash had to have been scared and watching out the window because as soon as I stepped out, he came outside yelling.

"April, what the fuck is you doing coming over here like this? We thought we was getting hit by the Feds!"

I wanted to tell him they would probably warn him first, but I knew I had to play nice. Before I responded, I looked around and realized that there was no way to tell that the season was changing. The grass that was in some of the yards was already brown, and there were no trees to see the leaves change colors. I was so grateful that my kids got to experience the small things, and that eased my mind. "Calm down. This just how we move when we on business."

"Why didn't you call first? You trying to make my spot hot or something?" Cash asked.

"Where do you want to talk?" I asked, ignoring his question.

He looked down the block before saying, "Let's go inside, but can y'all at least unblock the street?"

Nobody paid his words any attention. We just waited until some of the guys went and searched the house and kicked everybody out before we went in.

"Okay, Princess, you showed the hood how much power you got. So, let's get for real."

I took a seat on the couch with Bishop right beside me. Bull, Miracle, and three other security members remained standing. "If you want to be real, I got other stuff to be doing instead of being here."

"April, chill. Let's get this done and move around," Bishop said before I could speak my mind.

"Okay, Cash, you know you never were supposed to be out here like this, especially after what you did to get Mommy and Daddy locked up. Personally, I want you out the way, but Daddy wants me to give you a chance, and my king gave Daddy his word, so I'm going to make you an offer. and it's on you to take it or not."

"I talked to Dolla, and we didn't need to go through him to get an understanding, Princess. We can make a good team and take shit over," Cash suggested.

"You got one thing right, and that's we about to take over, but you ain't part of the *we*."

Bishop stopped Cash before he started talking again. "Look, homie, you drove down on me, ready to take my money, and when I didn't go for it, you took my hustle and even threatened me."

"I didn't know who you were to my niece," Cash said, trying to defend himself.

"That shit shouldn't even matter. All you were thinking was about yourself. Just like when you let your own brother go down." Bishop's voice was beginning to give away his anger. "I was a young nigga in the game, and you tried to get down on me when you had the power. So now that I got the power, I'm going to return the favor, but you don't have a choice. I'm taking all the blocks that you thought you owned. That means charging dues for blocks is over; you can't give or take no blocks from nobody. All of that shit is dead."

I wanted to start clapping because I didn't expect Bishop to get on him like that. I wished we could've just left it at that, but I knew Bishop was going to keep his word.

"What part of the game is that? I know Dolla didn't set it up like that." Cash was looking at everybody like somebody was about to help him.

"It's the part that you put in it, but I'm not the same kind of nigga as you. I'm going to give you a chance. So, you can eat too, but I swear on everything that I stand for and love that if you play any kind of games, I'm going to send niggas at your head from every way." I didn't know where that side of him came from, but I could tell that Bishop wasn't playing by his tone.

"It didn't have to come to this, but it got to be worth me letting everything go."

"You getting shit fucked up. We are taking shit, and the only reason you getting something is because of Bishop. So, you better be happy to be getting anything," I spoke, letting Cash now what was up. I was hoping that he said something crazy because I would've been happy not giving him shit.

"Look, I'm going to let you keep the area you got right here because you put work in. For the work, I'm giving Dolla five bricks every month that goes to you. I really don't want to be doing business with you, so I'm only going to sell you enough to eat with your family. I'll sell you another five bricks a month for twenty each. Money due up front for three months, and that's the only time we'll have anything to do with you."

Cash put his head down as Bishop was talking, and when he looked up, I could see the defeat on his face. "It really doesn't look like I got much of a choice, and it's time for the next person to take over." Cash looked at me, and I could tell he was salty. "I'm happy that it's you, Princess."

We all got up to leave, but before I left out the door, I turned my head and said, "For your sake, I hope you don't fuck up, but knowing you, I know you will... I'll be waiting. Oh, and one more thing. There's a new queen so stop all that princess talk."

The only thing that could have made that moment better was if I didn't have to give him shit, but I still walked away happy.

CHAPTER TWELVE

Bishop

I KNEW THAT WE WERE TAKING A LOT MORE ON OUR PLATE, AND WE needed to be organized in all our movements, so before bringing anything to the table, I gave everybody a task within their position. I did a lot of driving around, just to get the lay of the land. I wanted to see how other niggas were running their blocks. I knew which areas were really on something; I made a list of ones that had control on their block but was out there, the ones that were on some reckless shit, and the blocks that were so careful that you could barely tell what they had going on.

I remembered Hectic telling me they had a few connects within the Chicago Police Department, so I asked if he would be able to get me a list of the hotspots for drug arrests and only active investigations. He told me he would, but it would be better if I got to know them myself. I told him that I'd think about it. I knew it probably would be a good piece to have, but I knew that I'd never take him up on that offer.

When the day finally came for us to sit down and talk about everything, I was already seated at my spot at the table when the rest of them came in. I was ready to get straight to business, but April asked if she could say something first.

She stood back up and walked to my side and put one hand on my shoulder. When she cradled her belly with her other hand, I knew what it was before she spoke. "I didn't want to speak too soon, but Bishop is about to be a new daddy and uncle again."

I pulled her face down and gave her a kiss. I was about to thank her when the uncle part hit me. I turned to Blacky. "You too?"

He was smiling and nodded his head. "Let's just pray that it's a girl. Everybody know we don't need another kid,"

"Don't trip. I'm going to put another in April if it's not." April told me that she wanted to stop at four, but I had to mess with her. The way she responded let me know she meant it.

"He got me fucked up. If he plan to have another baby, he better hope his baby mama is with it because my tubes getting tied after this one," April announced.

"Yeah, I'm happy for all y'all, but none of y'all need more kids, with your wife or Amanda. They ass always hitting my pockets, knowing they don't need shit," Corn said.

"That's your problem for being so soft with them." I laughed at him.

"It's not a problem. Did you see the numbers that we've been pulling in, and do you know how shit is about to take off?"

"Yeah, that's what I want to talk about. We got a lot more shit to worry about now. So, tell me what you came up with."

Corn pulled his phone out and looked at it for a minute. "Okay, it seem like we was thinking along the same line. I wanted to see how the blocks moving. I saw you a few times, then when I asked Kayla to help me put together a map of what we control, she told me about some papers you got. So, once we're through with that, I really just need to see who we got to be careful with."

I cut in. "Yeah, I was going to tell you to cut them off."

"Can't do that, baby. I know this is your shit and not Daddy's, but I used to hear him say that you always need the fuck ups. They will draw the heat away from us," April spoke up.

"Plus, as long as they're buying and we know how to handle them, then our risk is minimum. And I know it's the least of our worries since we're not exposed. Understand that if they're not eating then they could start robbing our people or worse, they can start hustling on our blocks and make them hot. Best thing is to let them do them right where they're at," Corn added.

When Corn saw that I didn't have anything to say, he continued. "So, I thought about how to cut down our interaction with all these small-time niggas that's been stuck on buying a key or two, and I figured that since they don't got to pay block fees no more, they got some wiggle room."

He looked down at his phone again. "The way I see it, ten bricks at twenty thousand each shouldn't be a hard reach, and we throw in a brick of our own." He looked at April as he said the next part. "And they sell it for us and give us fifty thousand of that. Nothing is free in the trenches. If they work for it, then they'll appreciate it more."

We all turned to see what April's response would be. She closed her eyes and moved her head side to side before she looked back at us. "If they do it right, then it's like we're splitting the profits off of it, similar to how Daddy did it."

To be clear, I asked her, "You're good with that?"

"Yeah, it's fair."

I turned back to Corn to see what else he had, and he said, "This ain't a move to be made overnight, so what I'm going to do is tell guys to start stacking because shit will be changing soon. We probably play it by ear but six months to a year."

"That sounds about right. I'm not rushing shit as long as we got order. Blacky, what you got?"

"Before I get to that, let me add that we need to keep in mind that these blocks and niggas we dealing with got gang ties," Blacky said. "The reason that Cash was able to do what he did was due to his status in his gang. You better believe that he wasn't about to play them games with the gangstas on Jackson and California or none of the Breeds' blocks. Corn, you know it."

I understood what he was saying, but it didn't matter to me. "I hear you, and if you or Corn can use y'all affiliation to our advantage, then go ahead, but as a whole, we ain't getting involved in that shit. I'm good on that, and it's not about to dictate how we move."

"It's not like you need to join a gang, even though it'll give you a lot more power, which I know you're not looking for, but you got to understand that the gangs make up and run the streets at the end of the day."

"I get that, but it's not going to change how I move."

Corn got back in the conversation. "I get what Blacky is saying because we need to keep in mind that each gang got a set block, and they not about to come off them like that."

"We don't need the block, and we ain't worried about blocks if you ask me. Yeah, we got to keep shit in order, but that should be easy if money is being made."

"True, but this ain't the old west side of Chicago where we were known for getting money. We still doing that, but the murder rate keeps jumping up or passing out south and over east." Corn knew all the crazy details of shit. "So, we need to get the focus back on money."

April cut in. "Y'all failing to realize one thing. I was born into the top family of all this shit, and my daddy just made me queen of it. I know that's a little girl's fantasy that I'm living out, but we need to use that to our advantage. If Cash was able to get away with all the bullshit he was on then use y'all brains. The streets gone fuck with us with or without the gang shit."

Nobody said anything for a while, and I knew that this wasn't within my grip, so I did what was best. "I trust y'all, so I'm going to leave it in y'all hand. I won't vote on nothing concerning that topic since I'll probably see more bad than good each time. Just don't lock us in where one side or the other feel we're on their side, cool?" Everybody nodded and I moved on. "Now, Blacky, back to you. What you got?"

"Like everything, nothing is to be rushed, especially bringing somebody within our folds. I did put a lot of thought into the whole process more than the people. I want to see if they can first run a joint. That shit ain't easy. Then, can they be trusted with money and moving smart? I made a list of shit that might work, but who the fuck knows? A nigga can turn out like me or you, or they can turn out like Lil' Tone."

Blacky knew our street personnel best, and I wanted him to put together a list of niggas that had that go in them. "So… did you come up with anybody?"

He shook his head. "And I really wasn't trying. It's one nigga that I would stamp, but he got another year left in the joint."

Not trying to stay stuck on it, I turned to April. "What you looking at?"

She started laughing. "Boy, I had three of your kids already. I know you ain't about to let me do what I want to do right now. So, I'm looking at a lot of finger pointing shit like that, but you better believe by next year, my plan will be like no other."

She had me there. "Love you too, queen."

I didn't think I got what I wanted out of that meeting, but I did learn that I was moving too fast and needed to slow down. We hadn't had any situations where any of them agreed with me, and I always wondered how it would play out, and I was thankful that it didn't come down to anybody yelling or getting mad.

HAVING another kid on the way, being married, and being the head of a big drug operation was a lot to handle, but I knew that everything I did had a reason and benefit. So, I made sure I kept my reason in mind, and that made me think of Silk because he only wanted to make sure his family was straight. I liked how he was moving and wanted to put him in a better position.

I waited a couple of months, just to watch him and make sure that when he started seeing more than pack money, he wouldn't start on dumb shit or slacking. He did none of that. If anything, he was going harder, and I knew that I was doing the right thing.

I knew that I would find him on Washington in the alley. Since I didn't let April and Lucky around drugs while they were pregnant, I had to slide over there just to check on both the cook up and bag up spots.

I went to the building first and knocked on the door before opening it with the key that only me and April were supposed to have but now Baby D had. When I walked in, they had the music turned up, and I knew they didn't hear me. That irritated me, so I turned it off.

"Bishop, turn my music back on please!" Connie yelled from the kitchen.

I went in where I saw her and Baby D working. "What if I wasn't me? Y'all need to be on point. Do you know how many niggas would love to hit this spot?"

Baby D didn't stop what she was doing. "Well, the only people that got keys is me and you, so if anybody opens that door, it's a trick to it, but our job is to cook this shit up. That's on security to keep us safe. I'm trusting y'all that nobody will get in here, but if they do, I'm telling you now. I will give them everything, pack it up nice for them too." She stopped and looked at me. "They better not make it out the building with the drugs or their lives."

Baby D got back to working while Connie laughed.

"So, what, you come to help us or check on us?" Connie asked as she got to work.

"Just checking in, but if y'all need help, I can stay for a while."

"Naw, we got this, but if you want to grab us lunch, we'll love you a lil bit more than we already do."

"I got y'all. What y'all want?"

"If you buying, then a bitch ain't picky, but can you turn my music back on?" Connie spoke.

I saw all I needed, so I did as I was asked before walking out the house on my way to get their lunch. I did turn the music back on, and as I left out, I paid attention to the niggas posted up in the courtyard and on the sidewalk. I always just looked past them, knowing why they were there. The way they were dressed and acted, most would think they were posted up, selling drugs. The two things that gave them away was the big bulges of guns and their eyes didn't stop moving, watching everything.

I walked across the street and saw Silk talking to a female who I thought worked the weed spot. I went to the row house on Lotus and knocked on the door. It opened without anybody asking who it was.

"Hey, Bishop," Mona said.

I walked in and locked the door. "Y'all real comfortable over here, maybe a little too much."

"Hell naw, we might be too protected if anything."

"Why you say that?" I asked.

I turned around to see Mona standing there with her hands on her hips. "That nigga, Bull, got guns all over this block. I had my cousin drop some food off last week, and she said as soon as she turned down the street, her shit lit up with beams. She dropped the goods and got out of here, but they boxed her in down the street and wouldn't let her go til I gave them the okay."

I couldn't help but laugh. Bull said none of our houses would ever be touched again, and I saw he meant that shit — even if he was doing too much.

"Tell her I'm sorry that it happened. But you can't tell Bull nothing about running his security." I probably needed to talk to Bull about it though since an incident like that could make the spot hot if it got reported.

"At least I know I'm safe."

"We got you, but how is everything here?" I looked around and saw all ten desks with females bagging up. Three were for weed, five for rocks, and one for heroin since we only had a few dope lines. Mona's desk was the tenth.

"Since Lucky ain't here, I work nine hours and break for six. Then, I turn around and do that shit again. We keeping up with all the blocks, so I guess we good. Blacky said if we fall behind, he could cover the six hours as long as it's late nights."

"That's good. I'm here too anytime you need me."

"Good to know. Just next time, don't be planning to have babies at the same time."

"You know ain't no nigga plan that. Yeah, it was bound to happen at the honeymoon, but that was all April and Lucky."

"Well, don't let that shit happen again. This is real work right here, but the money is nice, so all is good."

"I bet. I'm going to slide, but just call if you need anything."

I left out and walked the alleyway. I stopped and looked around, just to take in the area where it all started. It was still moving like before. There were new faces, but in my eyes, I was still seeing us out there doing our thing. The biggest change was they knocked down all the row houses on Pine, and they were trying to do the same with the ones on Lotus. We just needed to buy them out, so we could keep them.

I walked over to Silk and watched him serve the few customers that were there. He moved quick, not taking a long time counting the money or fumbling with the bags, but what I didn't like was that he still had that female next to him. She had to be sixteen or so with a round, innocent looking face that had an upturned nose and pouty lips. Her skin was so light that she could pass as white. If it wasn't for her hair being thick and sandy brown, I would've thought she was white.

Silk walked over to me. "Big bro, what's the word?"

"Money as always." I gave him dap and looked over his shoulder at the female that followed him the few steps over. "What's good, shorty?"

"Nothing much." Her voice was soft, and I gave her another look over. She was about the same height as April when we first met. I wouldn't put her nothing over five foot, but she had a body that made me see why Silk had her close by.

I held my keys out to Silk. "Nigga, you think that you can drive my Hummer without fuckin' it up?"

He grabbed them. "Hell yeah, where we going?"

"Good. Let's go grab something from JJ's." We started walking away, but shorty stayed behind, so I said, "You not hungry or something?"

She smiled and followed behind us as we crossed the street. I got in the backseat as they got in the front. When Silk pulled off and I saw that he could drive, I sat back and thought about my options on how I was going to handle Silk. He was still on his hustle, so I would be okay with just putting him on, but he'd value and appreciate it more if I made him pay for his own shit.

Silk took a few extra blocks to get to JJ's Fish. When he parked, I gave him the order. I gave him a hundred and told him to buy him and his girl a meal. He got out, and she started to follow, but I stopped her.

"Stay here and keep me company." She closed the door and sat back in the seat but didn't say anything. "What's your name, shorty?"

"Tia. You're Bishop, right?"

"Yeah, I guess you heard about me," I spoke.

"Other than knowing that you run the streets and you messed with some of my girls and they talk too much, I know more than I care to." She laughed.

"Yeah, that's why I cut that shit out. I don't need my wife hearing that shit. But what's up with you and my boy?"

"Nothing yet, but I'm trying to get with him. I don't know if he's scared, or he just ain't feeling me."

"Naw, my boy ain't scared, and any nigga would be stupid not to be feeling you. He's just focused on his hustle, but don't trip. He gone see you."

"I wish that was true when he took that nasty ho on vacation with him," she spoke.

I had to laugh at that one. "He fucked up on that, but he'll make it up."

When he came back, I waited till we got back to the block and gave Baby D and Connie their food before I told him what was on my mind.

"Silk, I think it's time for you to move up and start getting some real money. You think you're ready for it?"

I thought he was going to die from choking, but when he stopped coughing, he said, "Hell yeah! I'm ready. What I got to do?"

I made up my mind right then not to give it to him the easy way. "Look, I'm going to give you your own block. So, you're going to need five thousand to get a brick, but you'll then owe me another five because I'll be charging you ten thousand a brick total."

"Man, I don't got that right now but give me a few weeks."

"I was saving for a car, but I got about five thousand if you need it," Tia said.

"For real?" I could tell that Silk was stuck that she was going to come off all that money.

"Yeah, but only if I can be your girl."

"I want that without the money. So, hell yeah!"

"Well, that worked out for everybody because with your new spot, you get a car. You need another three thousand to have it cooked up, three thousand more if you need it bagged up."

"So, you're telling me that I get my own block, a car, and a brick cooked and bagged up for sixteen Gs, and I can owe you what I don't got after my first flip?"

"Yeah, to start, but you better stack because when shit change, you're going to have to hold your own just like everybody else."

"I'm ready, big bro, real shit. I'm ready," Silk confirmed.

"I know. That's why I'm making this happen, but before you get started, take the weekend and show your girl a good time." I took some money out and gave it to him. "I'm going to call you first thing Monday, so I can set you up, and by Tuesday, it's going to be all you."

"I'll be ready." He had a big ass smile, and it made me realize just how young he was. "Which one of y'all gots your L?" I asked.

"I just got mine, baby," Tia said.

"Cool, then you drive and have fun."

I knew as soon as they pulled off, Bull was somewhere close, so I was waiting for him to pull up and get me, but my phone rang, and it was April.

"What's up, queen?"

"John, why the fuck is you playing with me? What bitch you got driving your Hummer?"

I tried not to laugh while saying, "Come pick me up out the alley and stop trippin'."

"Nigga, if you don't get that bitch out that truck, you going to see what trippin' is."

"April, that's Silk and his girl. I let them use the Hummer for the weekend."

Before I could say another word, April was coming down the street.

"Boy, you had me ready to kill something. These hormones got me going through it already," she said as soon as I closed the door.

I leaned over and gave her a kiss before I said, "It ain't shit, but you just confirmed we're having another boy."

"No, we ain't. Why are you saying that?"

"The first thing is that you're still barely showing. If it was a girl, you would've been talking about your feet hurting. When you were pregnant with Junior, your ass was super moody, just like your ass is now, but I still love you."

“I love you too, king.”

CHAPTER THIRTEEN

April

THE ONE PERSON THAT I KNEW WOULD TELL ME JUST HOW IT WAS, NO matter who was involved, was my mom. She was a down ass woman, which was where I learned it from, but Bishop was really testing me with this Cash shit. Without telling anybody except Miracle, I got a plane ticket and flew to where my mom was serving her time. I knew that I would get the advice I needed from her.

By the time I got to prison and was sitting at the table, waiting for her, I was still lost in my thoughts.

"Gurl, look at you! Damn, you look like I did back in my days. Come here and give me a hug."

My mommy came up to the table without me seeing her. Her voice made my head snap up. I walked up to her and hugged her and held her an extra second just to make sure I didn't start crying. When I pulled back, I said, "You're looking good too. If I didn't know better, I would think we were sisters instead of mother and daughter."

"What? You think I'm about to tell these bitches that you're my daughter? You my twin sister. That's my story, and I'm sticking to it."

For a second, I thought we were out, just kicking it, and not in a women's federal prison till one of the guards told us to sit at our table.

We sat down, and I said, "I'm sorry that I ain't come before now. Shit has been crazy, and I've been really busy."

"Baby, you been taking real good care of me, and I know how shit is out there, so don't worry about that and tell me why you traveled all these miles to talk to me by yourself because I know you still bringing my grandbabies and that sexy nigga here next month, right?"

"Yeah, they still coming, but I need to talk about Daddy."

"Let me guess. It got something to do with Cash?" she asked, clearly already knowing the answer.

I nodded, then I told her everything. She didn't stop me, and I ended up talking for over an hour.

She didn't say anything at first. Then, all of a sudden, she started laughing and said, "That's like some movie shit. Y'all out there doing really good."

"Yeah," I said in a flat tone, not really caring about that, and I was about to tell her.

Before I could get something else out, she asked another question. "And when did Dolla put y'all in touch with Top's son?"

"He didn't. Bishop already knew him, and we only found that out after the wedding."

"Small world. What about the connect? Is that from Dolla?"

"Naw, Daddy didn't help us with nothing. We worked and grinded for ours, and that's why I'm mad that we got to give dude anything. That's what I need help with. I want to get Daddy to leave him alone or get Bishop to see shit my way," I said.

She shook her head and frowned. "Look, baby, there is nothing that you can do to change Dolla's mind. That's his weakness. Bishop is your man, so I don't know how you got to work that angle, but don't think too much on it, just let it come to you, okay?"

"I guess, but I wasted the whole visit talking, and I didn't even feed you."

"Baby, just seeing and hearing that life is moving in the right direction for you is food to my soul. Plus, if you look this damn good after three kids and pregnant, then I got to be on top of my shit."

"If that's how I am going to be looking at forty-seven, then them bitches better watch out." I laughed, but she knew I was serious.

"Watch it! Don't be saying my age. But let's go take some pictures to get your daddy in trouble because he going to slap a nigga for looking at us too long."

I had some fun doing that with her, but I left still wondering how to get Cash out of the way.

———

Since I was pregnant and Bishop wouldn't let me do much, I was happy when he asked me to drive Looney's mom down to Menard to visit him.

When I got to her house, there were a bunch of guys standing on the corner. I damn near turned around. I wasn't scared, but I felt naked not having Miracle, Beauty, or my gun, and being somewhere I'd never been just didn't feel right.

As soon as I parked, they were all watching me, and I saw a few reaching for guns. I blew the horn, hoping I didn't have to get out and deal with these niggas when they saw that I was a female.

One of them, a bald headed, tall, and skinny Mexican came walking toward the car. I could tell he had his hand on his gun and was ready to use it. However, when I let the window down, I saw him relax.

"What you need, Mami?" he said when he got to the side of my car.

"I am just here to pick up somebody. She should be out soon."

"Oh, shit, my bad. I thought you was looking for some weed or something, but you're Bishop's girl, right?"

"His wife, April."

"I'm Juan, Looney's brother. I just got out the Feds, but I wanted to tell you how thankful and appreciative I am for all you've done for my brother. He said y'all the only reason he going to see his freedom again, and my ol' G said you paid the bills when shit got hard. That's the only reason that she still got the crib. I appreciate it because it's shit that I was supposed to be doing."

"Looney is family to Bishop, and we do whatever for family, so it ain't shit."

"Maybe not to you, but if you need something, just holla."

Even though I felt better knowing Juan was Looney's family, I was relieved when I saw their mom. She was a short, chubby, Mexican woman. Closing the door behind her, she came and got in the Infinity with me, and we got out of there. As we drove south, an eight-hour trip, I finally came up with a plan. I guessed the trip to see Mommy wasn't a waste. She told me that it'd come to me, and it did. I just hated that I couldn't talk about it with anybody close to me; they'd all shut it down.

I didn't feel comfortable asking Juan to help me, even though he offered. I knew that if it could be done, Looney would make it happen. I had to time it right, and I waited till Looney's mom went to the bathroom during the visit before I said something.

"You think you could get your brother to take care of some business for me?" I asked.

"With no questions asked, just say the word," Looney answered.

"I'll pay him to do it. It's dangerous, and he might need some help."

"April, don't trip on none of that. He the Inca, which mean he's the top brother for the hood, so if he says move, they move. Now, what's up?"

"Some slight shit but if I don't see him when I drop your moms off then give him my number and tell him to call."

"Okay. I got you," he assured.

It took a few weeks before I got the call from Looney's brother, and I'd thought for a second that he didn't want to get involved. We talked, and I agreed to meet him on his block to give him the full rundown of what I needed handled. Even though I knew everything was good, I still felt better having Beauty and my gun with me; especially being outside our area. Plus, knowing that Miracle was close by, I knew nothing would happen if Juan wasn't out there when I pulled up.

I got to his block and saw Juan and a bunch of guys posted on the corner. When he saw me pull up, he turned around, and I could tell he was putting his gun up before walking to my car.

"You could've kept your shit on you. I know I feel better with mine," I stated.

"It's not that. The more rounds out there the better. It's always wartime, especially since everybody knows I'm out."

"Well, I guess this the safest spot for you right now because if someone looks at my car wrong, they are going down."

"Pull around to the back of the house, so we can go in and handle what you came here for. My fault it took this long to call. Bro told me to let you know they went on lockdown, and that nigga just called me yesterday."

"Yeah, I was wondering what happened, but it's all good." I pulled around back, and when we got out, I let Beauty out, and Juan damn near took off running.

"What the actual fuck? That motherfucker was back there the whole time?"

"Yeah. She stays with me, and she knows how to stay in the cut," I confirmed.

"Do you breed her?"

"I never thought about it. I got her more for protection."

Juan led the way in the house. We came in right at the kitchen then walked into the room. As soon as we entered, I smelled the weed in the air. There was a mattress on the floor with some chairs along the wall and a big ass black beanbag in the corner. On the walls was a bunch of black and gold RIP shirts. I sat in one of the chairs with Beauty at my feet; Juan sat across from me on the mattress.

"Well, if you do, just keep me in mind. With that out of the way, what's the business you want to talk about?"

"I'll get to that, but besides gangbanging, what else you be on?"

"Same shit everybody else is on, trying to stay alive and get some money. Shit changed since I been gone, and it's a lot of new faces in the game, and while I'm building, I'm ready to go take what I want."

"I'll give you two bricks right now if you can take care of something for me, and that should solve both our problems," I spoke, thinking quickly.

"Two bricks and I'll kill the mayor. Just tell me who and it's done."

"It's a nigga named Cash from out west. To me, he ain't shit, but some of them still look at him like he's something, so it might be hard to get at him."

"But it's possible, right?" he questioned.

"Yeah, it's possible, but it's going to be in his area, so it's going to be more than just him."

"If you can come off two keys, then I know you want this done bad. Do you think you can get me a few choppas? AK-47s is my favorite."

"First, let me make the call to get these bricks for you. I'll have to talk to somebody else about the guns, but I'll get them for you." I called Corn and told him what to bring me, and as we waited, I gave Juan all the info he needed on Cash.

When Corn dropped the bricks off, I was happy he didn't ask any questions because I hated to lie. Juan could take himself, and I knew that I'd be able to get him to do shit that I didn't want our name on.

I told him that he'd get a call about the guns he wanted before I left. When I got down the street, I saw Miracle following behind me and pulled over. She hopped out her whip and got in the passenger seat in my car. I told her what I needed and knowing that she would figure out what I was on, I told her my plan. She didn't make anything of it. She got on the phone and was able to get three AKs without raising any flags. Driving off, the only thing that I had to wait on was for the streets to announce that Cash was dead.

CHAPTER FOURTEEN

Bishop

EVERY SHIPMENT THAT CAME IN WAS AT A NEW SPOT. WE DIDN'T WANT anyone getting comfortable with us being at one spot and robbing or calling the police on us. José and Jesus meant it when they said that they were going to keep me safe from going down. The driver only knew where to go at the last second, and me and Hectic were the only ones to know til we were ready for our other workers to come do their parts.

Today was my first time bringing Corn with me. He was the one selling weight for us, and I felt it'd be easier for him to have his own inventory separate from the row houses that did ours. We had just finished taking care of dropping everything off where it needed to be, and Corn wanted to show me how he wanted to start setting up the blocks between the ones we put our shit on, the ones we put up for our people to come up on, and the ones that were off limits. He explained that we weren't going to try to force anybody off their block, but if they weren't going to play by our rules, then all the blocks around them would have a bigger bag with better product, so their money would slow down til they got with the program.

We were on our way to the crib when Corn turned down the music and looked at me.

"Man, they're saying that they fucked Cash shit up last night. Like five of his guys got bodied, and niggas still fighting for their lives as we speak."

"That's fucked up. Did he get hit too?" I really didn't care one way or the other since he probably deserved whatever came his way.

"Naw, he got out the way in time, and other niggas got in front of him like he was the president or something."

"Do anybody know..." I stopped talking as I looked out the window, and I saw a face from the past.

"What up, homie? You know them?"

There wasn't many faces I had to remember off something bad, so I knew I wasn't tweaking, but to be sure, I told Corn to spin back that way. "I want to make sure that's who I think it is."

Corn's Lincoln Navigator was tinted up, so when we pulled up next to them, they couldn't see us. I knew for sure now that it was the same nigga that got down on me for Lil Tone selling dummy bags on his block. That was the first time I killed, and knowing he was still alive had me ready to kill again. I pulled my gun out and took the safety off. I was about to open the door, but Corn grabbed my arm.

"Hold up, bro. What you on?" I stopped, but before I could respond, Corn's phone got to ringing. When he picked up, I heard Bull on the other end, but I couldn't make out his words, only Corn's response.

"I don't know. Homie just told me to pull over, and now he ready to put his murder game down."

"Yeah, let's do that shit," I confirmed, ready to body a nigga.

My focus didn't leave from the nigga that I wanted til Corn hung up. "My nigga, look at me." I did, and he said, "Chill. Whatever it is, we gon fix it, but don't do no dumb shit." I didn't respond as he pulled off and drove a few blocks away.

We pulled in the gas station, and Bull jumped in the backseat and said, "What's to it?"

I hit the dashboard. "That bitch ass nigga robbed me and put his feet on me."

At the same time, they said, "When?"

"This was before Bull got on the team. Corn, you were locked up, and I was still fucking with Lil Tone's clown ass."

"Oh, that's when you shot them niggas. I remember, but I didn't know it was him. Dude is a good customer, but we can't let that go so put that call in, Bull."

As soon as I'd been released, I caught Corn up on everything that happened while he was locked up, and he remembered what I was talking about.

Bull was already dialing numbers, letting me know he'd heard enough.

Bull got out, and Corn left the gas station and pulled up to the corner opposite to the building they were posted up at. I was trying to think of his name the whole time, and it clicked when I saw him again: Buddy Lord. I had hoped that he was one of the two niggas that I killed when I shot up their block, but all these years later, he was going to pay for that shit. Knowing Bull, all seven niggas standing out there with him were going to die too.

We sat there and watched them standing against the wall of the apartment building. Another car was there that wasn't there the first time we pulled up. They didn't even know we were watching their every move.

"On some real shit, Bishop… I know dude got to go, but we on a whole different level than it was in them days, so we need to move like it," Corn spoke.

"So, you saying let that shit slide? I don't act like I'm a gangsta or none of that, but niggas need to know that I'm not to be played with. If it takes me to jump out this car and fuck dude up for people to realize that, then that's what it is."

"I'm not going to argue, but doing shit that way, you're making enemies. You might not know when you can get it done on the lowkey side, and nobody would even know. The streets will realize every time somebody play games with you, they'll end up dead, but nobody will be able to say if you did it or not."

I didn't have anything more to say. I understood what he said, but this was one thing I couldn't let go for some reason. I was willing to let Bull take care of it though as long as it happened.

"Look at them niggas. They won't even see it coming."

Corn's phone started ringing, and when he picked up, he listened then described what Buddy Lord was wearing. I looked around, knowing that they were coming. I saw the beams first. One of the niggas standing out there saw it too and tried running, but a small silver car pulled up and started letting them have it. My eyes went to Buddy Lord just as two niggas jumped out of a minivan and started shooting him. He was shot so many times his body was held up against the building until the shots stopped. When he dropped, another nigga ran up and shot him some more, overkilling him.

That shit took less than a minute, but it sounded like hundreds of shots went off, and all the niggas that were out there no doubt was dead. Corn tapped my shoulder. "It's that easy, homie. Use the pieces that you got and let them handle their part. You're too important to risk. Think about that. Now, let's slide before blue and white come shut this bitch down."

Pulling off, I looked at them laid out one last time and knew that Corn's advice was solid. A message like that would be felt all through the west side, and all I had to do was give the order.

Corn and I walked into April and Blacky watching the news that was talking about the shooting. I saw April's face go from nervous to relieved when she saw me. Normally when we had any kind of meeting, I was the first there to make sure the money was situated. So, I could see how us being missing in action would have her worried.

"Where y'all been at?" she asked.

"Some unexpected shit came up," I answered her while trying to listen to what the news said.

"Well, would you at least call if you're going to be late? That's not like you. You had me worried," April suggested. I could tell she had been anxious, and that was something I didn't want.

I knew what she was thinking because the news was saying it. They thought the Cash and west side shootings were related because of the kind of weapons used and the way the attacks happened. I would tell her that I didn't have anything to do with Cash and that we were the shooters in today's shooting, but it didn't seem like the right time. So, I got down to business.

"If y'all couldn't tell, money is really nice. Soon, we will be weighing our money instead of counting it. This time around, there will be an extra bag for everybody to give your main workers as a bonus."

Corn started talking after I finished. "Look, I've been looking at ways to clean up money, and I think we should get in the stripper game."

"I'm with it. I'll be Black Stallion." Everybody looked at Blacky, and when I saw he was for real, I started laughing so hard, and everyone joined it.

April was crawling out the room, trying to stop laughing. "Stop before this baby comes out."

Corn pointed at Blacky. "Ah, man, this nigga said Black Stallion like he was going to be a stripper."

Blacky was looking around, confused. "He said get in the stripper game, so what the fuck is so funny?"

"Nigga, he ain't talking about us being strippers." I was able to say that without laughing too hard as I sat back in my chair. "April, come on. We done."

When we were in this room, it was always business, and with so much going on, I thought we were laughing at Blacky thinking we would be strippers, but I knew I was letting some tension out.

"Fuck it. Get on the table and show us what you got Black Stallion," April said when she came back in the room, causing us all to laugh.

When we calmed down, Blacky said, "Okay, y'all got me on that one, but can we please get back to business? I'm done being y'all joke."

Corn said, "Alright, so check this. My girl was telling me…"

"Hold up, say that again." April interrupted him.

"All I got to say was that my girl was telling me."

"That's what I thought. You never claimed nobody as your girl but continue."

"So, she was breaking it down how a stripper or call girl can self-report on their taxes since it's no way to tell how much they really make because they get paid off tips in so many words. She said one of her girls be cleaning her man's drug money up like that."

"So, we can use our wives to clean up a little money, but would it really be worth it?" I tried to do the math really quick on how much we could slide through, and it didn't seem like that much given how much we were making.

"I mean, we can do that too, but first, we can buy this strip club in Harvey, which will bring us in money anyways, but we can add drug money to our earnings. Most of the bitches there don't know shit about taxes, so we give them a hundred thousand over the year, and we take eighty from that."

"I'm not going to lie. That shit sounds good to me, but I'm not agreeing to it until Kayla gives it the okay. We're going to really have to trust these females because that kind of money isn't something that we can take an L on," April said. In the end, she knew that she would be the one dealing with them if we agreed to go through with this idea.

"That's cool, but I'm going to go on and start working on getting this club because homie got other offers, and I think it's worth the investment. I think we can clean about fifty thousand or so every week. Plus, homie that's selling it said he knows how to do the paperwork where it looks like we're paying the whole cost in cash out the bank, but really the sale is more. The rest can be paid under the table, and he not even putting that much of a tax to it. I would rather take the risk and figure it out as we go over missing out on this."

CHAPTER FIFTEEN

Bishop

I WAS DOWN WITH EVERYTHING THAT MADE US MONEY OR CLEANED UP all the drug money we were making. When it came down to it being able to turn at least two and a half million a year, I was quick to jump on board.

The spot was set up where we didn't have to do anything. We kept all the people who wanted to stay except the bouncers; Bull wasn't going for that. We all met Corn's girl, Moriah, but were introduced using our real names. I thought we were all surprised that she was plus sized, but she was still bad with it, and if the baby dreads and dark skin wasn't telling enough, as soon as she started talking, you knew that she was Jamaican. We had already talked about her role if we were comfortable with her, and we all agreed that she could manage the club, but she wouldn't have anything to do with our street business.

April hung out with her for over a month before giving her the okay, and as soon as she got put into play, she showed her worth. She had the club popping every night with different themes, and it was turning out to be more than Corn saw.

What I didn't see were niggas being stupid enough to stick us up while we were in our spot.

With the kids over at Amanda's house for the weekend and everybody else out doing their own thing, I put work to the side and was thinking about ordering out when Corn called. He had Moriah on a three-way call and told her to tell me what she heard. I listened for the next five minutes as she told a story that I wasn't feeling one bit.

I got up from the recliner I was sitting in when the call came in. "So, they were going to set up a deal to kidnap me and then rob all our spots? How did you know who I was?"

She answered. "I didn't know who you were. If they didn't say Corn was your righthand, I would've minded my own business, just as I've done many other times when I heard them planning a lick."

"You know these niggas?" I asked, not in the mood for any bullshit.

"They come to the club almost every week, and they're always planning to rob somebody, but they said that if they can pull this off, they can leave the state and be all the way on wherever they go."

"How many of them is it, and where they from?" I wanted to know something about them before I made a move.

"Normally, it's six of them, but one isn't here, and I think they're from the Heights."

"Cool. Hit bro up if they leave. Corn, I need to make a call but get back at me in a few minutes."

I ended the call and put my plan into play with one call.

"Bull, we got some niggas planning to kidnap me, and I'm about to go meet them."

"Nigga, is you stupid or just trying to make my job hard?"

"Naw, they at the club, and it's the best place to catch them, so I'm going to close it down, but first, I want you to be in place because they not leaving of their own will, and I want them dead." I laughed, knowing Bull was already on his way to see what was up. One thing about Bull, he didn't play about me, and niggas were going to find that out the hard way.

"I'll take care of that, but don't leave the house till I get there, just give me ten minutes."

"Ten minutes, nigga? You slipping because Superman would be here in five minutes or less."

"Bet. Put on a vest and leave in three."

When Corn didn't call after I left the crib, I sent him and Blacky a text, telling them to meet me at the club. I knew Bull was somewhere he could see me, but he told me that if I saw somebody following me, then it wasn't him.

I was right around the corner from the club when Corn called.

"What's good, big bro?" I answered.

"Shorty called and said their last guy just got there, and there's a group of other niggas that don't look right," he spoke.

I knew the group of other niggas were probably sent by Bull. "Alright, tell her to send a bottle to each of them from the owner and send them a dancer too. After that, have her send everybody out the back, so we can have a surprise party."

"How long till you pull up?" he asked me.

"Like five," I replied.

"We ready."

By the time I pulled up, cars were leaving the parking lot. I didn't even bother to park. I pulled up to the front door and got out.

Corn and Blacky were there, waiting, and out of nowhere, Bull was at my side.

"So, what's the plan?" Blacky asked loud enough to be heard over the music as we walked in the club.

"Really just trying to see if we can trust shorty. I'm not worried about them having no bangas if our people did their jobs. I want to see these niggas' faces before they die."

I knew that I was going to hear about it later. I knew I could've had everything taken care of without leaving the crib, but these niggas had plans to take my life.

I didn't bother with my gun since I knew everybody else had one. I ran up the stairs to the V.I.P. rooms and walked in the one they were in. They were too focused on the pussy to even see me. The room had all black everything with dimmed lights.

A nigga sitting across from the door had a female dancing on him. He was in his glory, and I was trying to see if I'd ever seen him before. He must have felt me staring at him. "What the fuck, foe?"

"Oh, shit!" another one said when he looked up. He looked like he'd seen a ghost. He must've known who I was. He pushed the stripper that was dancing on him off and tried standing up.

"Nope! Sit yo ho ass down." Bull stepped up and put a pump in his face.

All the dancers took off out the door, and beams started lighting up all the niggas' faces.

"Damn, foe, what you on?" another one of them asked, looking like he was about to shit his pants.

"I heard y'all was looking for me so here I am." Looking at these niggas, I could tell they were about bullshit. They were in a strip club dressed in all black. If I didn't know they already had a plan to get me, I would think that they came to the club just to hit licks.

"Foe, we don't even know you. We just here trying to have a good time. We ain't on none of that bullshit."

"Last time I heard, you niggas was planning to kidnap me, but y'all so dumb some of y'all don't even know who I am," I said when I realized that some of them really didn't know who I was.

"He that bitch nigga, Bishop, from out west," one of the guys said, recognizing me. As soon as he said it, Bull split his shit, slapping him with the pump across the face.

"But this bitch nigga gonna make your mama cry." My phone started ringing, and I hit ignore without even looking at who it was.

"Yeah, but without these niggas behind you, your ass won't be shit, and all you would be doing is telling your bitch to send us that bag to get your bitch ass back."

"But they are behind me, and the best part is that your lil bitch told me what y'all was on. She's going to die right beside you too." I didn't trust people outside of my family to start with, so I had to throw something out there to see if Moriah was really involved. Either she was going to beg for her life or I would see that they really knew we had all the info.

"What bitch?" It seemed to click who I was talking about. "I told y'all that bitch was coming back too much and listening hard every time."

It seemed like all the phones started ringing, and this time, I answered.

"What?!"

CHAPTER SIXTEEN

April

"WHAT?!" I COULD NOT BELIEVE THIS NIGGA SENT ME TO HIS DAMN voicemail then to answer like that. I wanted to pop off on him, but this baby's head was halfway out, and I couldn't argue.

"Bishop, the baby is on the way. You need to hurry up and meet us at the hospital."

He didn't answer me. I could tell he covered the phone, but I heard what he said, and a chill ran through my body and made me worry about him more than myself being in labor.

"I got to go but take them somewhere and smoke them all. Make that shit bad too." I heard him say before letting me know he was on his way.

"April, put the phone down and listen to this man. You about to have this baby in this ambulance because we ain't making it to the hospital for real now!" Mama Kelly yelled.

"Mama, something bad is happening. Call them and make sure all of them are okay."

"Hush, girl, and give me another grandbaby. That's who I need you to focus on."

"Okay, April, I have your doctor on the phone, and she said it's safest for us to deliver right now, so we're going to find a safe place to park and get through this. Are you okay?" the paramedic asked.

I wanted to yell at him and everybody else.

"I want Bishop here, and he wants to be here when the baby is born," I cried, not wanting to have our baby without him.

"Sorry, but unless he's in the car behind us then that's not possible." Lucky was able to make it to the house and was driving behind us. None of the guys were able to be reached until this point.

It was clear to me that this labor was different from all the other times. I remembered hearing it cry and making it to the hospital, but after that, I went blank.

———

BEEP. *Beep. Beep.*

I woke up in the hospital. I was scared to open my eyes and see Bishop hooked up to any machines. I remembered how it was for Blacky, and I knew I couldn't take that.

I tried to say his name, but it only came out as a moan. I could barely open my mouth.

"April." I heard Bishop's voice, and I felt like I was dreaming. "Mama Kelly, go get the nurse and let them know she's waking up." Bishop grabbed my head and held a cup to my lips. I could barely keep my head up, even with his help, but I took a sip of water.

I slowly opened my eyes and saw him standing over me.

I reached up to him, and he smiled. "Welcome back, queen. There's somebody waiting to meet you."

"What's wrong with me?" I found my voice and asked him, but before he answered, the nurse was checking me over.

"She might need a little more rest from the stress of everything, a sedative and some water, but everything is all good."

He gave me water, and I asked again. "What's wrong with me, Bishop?"

"You had our baby. They said it was too much for you. So, they gave you something to put you to sleep, but you're all good."

"But something happened. I remember."

"Damn, that must have been some good shit they gave you. You had our baby. That's all, and I'm all good."

It all came back to me. "Bishop, I heard you on the phone. What happened?"

"Right now, you need to rest, but we'll talk about that later. Are you ready to meet our baby?" As he said that, everybody walked in the room.

I saw Corn and Blacky and knew that I had been tripping before and that everything was really okay. That thought was enough to relax me as I fell back to sleep.

"APRIL, you were tweaking super hard. Mama Kelly said you were trying to push our son back in yourself, saying you wouldn't have him till I got there."

It took me a few days of rest at home before I felt like talking about anything. I didn't leave the house, but I paid attention to how they were moving, and I could tell that there was tension.

Bishop came in our bedroom and sat at the foot of the bed while I was feeding our baby. He put my feet on his lap and started rubbing them.

We had another baby boy like Bishop had said. Bishop said he wanted all of his sons to have his name, so we named him Jon, but Corn started calling him BJ. He said it meant Baby Jon, but he said Bishop Junior a lot too.

I tried to laugh it off. "I don't know what that was they shot me with, but we need to bag that shit up and sell it."

"And if you weren't acting crazy enough, Lucky was set on having her baby that same day, even if it meant cutting it out. I'm just happy she had her damn girl. But forget all that. How you feel?"

I had it on my mind since I heard him say those words over the phone, and I knew that it had to be something that wasn't settled yet because I could tell the difference in how he was acting.

I finally decided to cut right to it. "I would be better if you stopped hiding things from me and tell me what's going on with you. I know something happened that night I had Baby Jon. I heard you order Bull to kill some niggas, and that tone was not you, so I want to know what happened."

I could see that he thought about it before speaking. "Moriah heard some niggas talking about grabbin' me and trying to make you pay to get me back. I really think they had plans to kill me."

"Wait, slow down. The first thing I want to know is how did she know your name?" We all knew not to mix her with our street business, so the only nickname she knew was Corn, and she called Blacky "B" since he didn't like anybody calling him Josh.

"She said it wasn't till she heard them say Corn's name that she paid attention and thought to call and ask if he knew somebody named Bishop, and then we went from there."

"Okay, so how did y'all find the niggas after that?" I asked.

"Shit, they was planning it at the club, and we caught them before they left."

"At the club?" I gave him a look, so he knew how stupid I thought that was.

"Yeah, but nobody was there but us. We told everybody that we were having a V.I.P. party. Then, they were taken somewhere else after you called, and I had to leave."

"So, that's done with because I can't lie, Bishop, my mind went somewhere else when I heard you say that. Maybe it was the shot they gave me, but this shit ain't worth our family. So, either you keep that nigga that I heard over the phone on standby or we walk away." I knew what I was asking, but I didn't know what I was going to get.

I didn't expect the answer to come the way it did.

"I see now that being just about money and having straight killas on the team don't get you respect in the streets, but moving on, niggas won't be able to say I'm only a gangsta because of the niggas that I got behind me. I'm going to keep moving smart, but niggas going to know not to play with me."

"Always remember that whatever it is, I'm going to be right beside you."

"Ain't no doubt about that."

CHAPTER SEVENTEEN

April

I walked in the boardroom to find Corn, Blacky, and Bishop sitting at the table. Corn had Mama Kelly come get my baby from me so that I could focus on what he had to talk about.

"Corn, I swear this better be life or death important because my baby needs me right now and having somebody come take him from me ain't a good look." As soon as the words left my mouth, I saw Miracle and Bull standing in the corner. That alone let me know that something real was happening.

"Yeah, April, it's on that level. And now that you're here, I can let everybody know what's up," Corn spoke, waiting for me to take my seat. "I got a call from one of our customers, asking me why he need to pay for his blocks again. He is talking about how he would have to drop a couple of blocks and cut his order in half."

Bishop damn near jumped out of his chair and yelled. "So, why the fuck is he paying for blocks? That ain't the way we moving, so what the fuck is going on?"

"You're acting like this shit is our doing. I deal with that shit too. This my first time hearing this shit, and ain't no doubt none of our blocks had to deal with nobody coming talking about paying dues," Blacky said with anger in his voice.

"Aye, chill. That shit ain't on us. I went to other spots to see how many more was dealing with the same shit, and after going through like five, I knew what it was, but I asked just to be sure." Corn looked at me, and I knew what he was going to say before he said it.

"April, your uncle, Cash, is back on bullshit."

"First, miss me with the uncle shit. I told y'all that we should have just cut that nigga off. So, don't act surprised now that the snake bit you. Now, we have to kill the animal that we made real fat."

"And that's not a problem, April. We chose to do what we did, and we got to deal with it. We got to do what we got to do and get that nigga out the way. I personally feel you should handle it since he's your blood."

"Hell naw! Nigga, you lost your mind if you think I'm about to let my wife go do something like that. Bro, I don't even know what would make you say some shit like that," Bishop shot. It was clear that he didn't agree with his suggestion.

"She won't be by herself. I'm with her. I'm not asking her to pull the trigger or nothing. I just want her to set it up and make the call, so it's a family thing. Trust me on this one, homie."

I had Juan already in play, and maybe with Corn's help, I could finally get this shit done and have Cash out the way. I made it so Bishop couldn't argue about me being involved.

"If I can't do something like this, then my vows weren't shit, and I will feel better telling my daddy that it was my call to take his brother out."

Even if he was thinking about saying no, he simply nodded. "Get this shit done tonight or tomorrow or we going over there and I'm blowing his shit back in front of all his guys." He didn't wait for a response before he got up and left.

It was quiet for a minute before Bull began speaking. "If y'all going to be on shit like this instead of letting me and mine do our jobs then at least come in and train more for it. Miracle, don't leave her side. Corn, somebody will be on you and Blacky till I feel comfortable with this situation. In less than three months, we have had two incidents where lives were lost. Who knows what's going to come from this, but please get it done so all our asses don't end up in jail with a hundred bodies." He got on his phone and walked out.

"I guess that's that. April, let's ride, so we can get this done. It feels like our heads are on the line right now," Corn said.

I didn't need much, so I was ready fast and called Juan as we got in Corn's Lincoln. I thought about telling Corn, but as soon as we turned in traffic, he turned to me.

"Sis, I told you if you wanted to make a move on Cash, I'd ride with you, didn't I?"

"Yeah. The first time when I went to holla at him about them blocks."

"So, what you didn't believe me or something?"

"Why wouldn't I?" I looked at him and knew he was serious.

"I don't know, but I keep my ear to the streets, and while Cash is a grimy ass nigga and so many niggas got reason to want him dead, none would be Mexican. Then, I got to putting two and two together. You got homie that I dropped them bricks off to to do this, but he missed three times and got Cash running scared."

I didn't see any reason to deny it, but I wasn't about to explain anything. "Yeah, but he did what I knew he would do. So, he gave us a reason to do it anyways," I said.

"April, if we run these streets, then we don't need a reason. If we want something to be done, then we do it. That nigga might be stupid, but he ain't fucking up that kind of paper. I came up with the story for Bishop, and I got niggas that's going to back it up just in case he went to check. All the same, we need to finish this shit, so we don't make no dumb mistakes."

He was right, but my mind went to how we were going to get him out, so we could get it done.

"I still want Juan to take care of this, but I'm going to call Cash and tell him I need his help. If he really wants to prove himself, I think he'll come asap."

Corn was focused on the road but nodded. "Yeah, that should work except I don't want you out there when shit happens. If we don't have to get our hands dirty, then I'm good with it."

"We can have him hit down the block from where we're supposed to meet."

We talked it all out until we got up north, then we went over it again with Juan. After making sure everybody was ready to do their part, I called Cash and laid it on thick, so he felt that I would owe him, especially since he was getting fucked up every time he popped out the house.

I knew that he wouldn't want to be away from his guys, but I didn't want them to know he was coming to see me. I didn't want people to know or think I had something to do with setting him up.

I waited for him to call, so I could give him the location of where to meet me. The spot was in the parking lot of an old shut down store, but it was far enough from the street to where it wouldn't bring attention to us sitting there. The main thing was that it was only two ways in or out. Once Cash pulled in one way, I would leave out the other way, and Juan's people would block him in and hopefully take care of the business this time around.

Before we left out, I had to make sure Juan knew that he had to get it done this time.

"Look, I'm giving him to you this time. You can't miss or he'll know I set him up and was behind y'all shooting at him before," I said.

He was high off sniffing coke and looked like he was ready to go to war with the world.

"Don't even worry. I'll chop his head off just so you know it's done."

"Naw. Leave that shit to the cartel, but make sure everybody that comes with him is dead too. He shouldn't think it's a hit, so if it's a reason that he's not there, we going to go hit his house."

We thought about nearly everything and had some of Bull's guys on post at his house, ready to knock him off there if need be.

I liked that Corn stayed in the cut for the most part and let me handle everything. He waited till we were at the meet-up spot, and after an hour of waiting, I was ready to call Cash and see where he was.

"You do that, and he won't show up. He's scared, so right now, it don't matter if you're blood or not. If you seem too thirsty, that shit going to run him off. He going to be here, don't trip," Corn spoke, stopping me from calling.

We waited almost another two hours before my phone rang. I

thought it was going to be Bishop, but when I saw that it was Cash, I thought he was backing out, and we were going to have to get him another way.

I answered. "I'm waiting on you, Unk."

"I'm pulling up right now; do you see me?"

I saw three cars turning in the open space where I was sitting. I knew that none of them were going to make it from here, but if I really needed him, why would he have come like this? I had to take my feelings out of it and find out which one of the cars he was in.

"Yeah, I see you but tell them other cars to fall back. I don't need niggas in my business." I saw Corn texting the info to Juan, and as soon as I saw it was Cash in the car that pulled up, I sped off.

"Princess, what the fuck is going on?" I could hear the fear in his voice, and I knew he could see what was about to happen. "Don't do me like this. We family!"

"You ain't my family. My daddy might be blind to your bitch ass shit, but you're not about to make another dollar off the family that I built for myself after you took my first family." I looked in the rearview and saw Juan riding up, starting to light up the car that Cash was in.

I didn't hang up the phone, and I heard bullets hitting parts of the car, but every time a bullet hit Cash, he made a noise that would've made my stomach weak if it was somebody else. But knowing that it was Cash and that we were finally getting rid of his dirty ass, I pulled off.

I kept my ear to the phone, and after all the shooting stopped, I heard Juan talking to a few of his guys in Spanish, then they let off more shots before it got quiet for good, so I hung up.

From the time I heard Corn say Cash's name, and especially after finding out that he did Bishop wrong, I knew I was going to kill him. I thought that it was going to be hard to get Bishop to go with it after he gave my daddy his word, but now, the only person I didn't want to find out was my daddy.

CHAPTER EIGHTEEN

April

I KNEW IF I SKIPPED THE FUNERAL, IT'D BE A LOT OF TALKING. THE streets were saying somebody had to have set him up, and it had to be somebody that he trusted, but nobody was saying my name, and I didn't want to give them reason to start.

I knew Bishop didn't like the whole idea either, but he saw the point, and since nobody knew who did it, all of Cash's guys thought someone would come shoot the funeral up. We told them we would have security set up. They knew how deep we came through their spot, and we weren't to be played with, so they felt safe with that.

We also knew the police were going to be there, expecting something to go down but trying to figure out who everybody was being that Cash was still considered a high-ranking member of a gang, so his funeral brought out many people that had their hands in the streets.

As we were leaving, I saw a group of cops coming my way. When they got to me, they showed me their badges.

"April Thompson, I'm Detective Brook with the Chicago Police Department. We're sorry about what happened to your uncle, and we're working hard to find out who is behind his murder along with the six other people. I know it's not a good day for you, but do you mind coming in and answering a few questions?" There were three of them; the one that spoke to me was heavyset and wore a suit that was a size too small.

I knew what they wanted to know. We had talked about it with the lawyer already, and he felt that I could go in without saying that I wanted my lawyer.

"Okay, but you'll have to tell me where to go because, no offense, but I would like to go my whole life without getting in the backseat of a police car."

"Well, you're not a suspect in any way, so if you're ready now, you can just follow us." He said what I wanted to hear. As long as they didn't read me my rights, then they weren't on to me.

"We can do that." When I got to the car with Bishop driving, I said, "I know what I'm supposed to do but still call the lawyer and have him call me in thirty minutes and tell him to say that my uncle's people called him."

"If you don't feel comfortable doing it, just say so, and you don't have to."

"It's not that. I just want to get it over. We made a plan, and the lawyer said it would work if I stayed to the script. If they're not done or close to it by then, then they got too many questions. Him calling with that message will be my way out."

"Then do it."

I didn't know if that meant he would do as I asked or not, but we didn't talk for the rest of the ride to the violent crime's police station headquarters on Harrison and Kedzie.

I followed three officers to the interview room, and they offered me something to drink before we got started.

Once we were seated around the table, the same officer spoke. "So, as you know, we're investigating the murder of your uncle, who is known by Cash in the streets, and six of his associates. Before we get started, I'm letting you know this interview is being recorded. Is that okay with you?"

"I don't have a problem with that."

He went in his folder and slid a card with his name and number on it, Detective Brook.

The G.I. Joe looking one did the same and said, "I'm Detective Lowe, also with the Chicago Police Department."

I could tell the last guy was a federal agent; his suit was nicer, and he was more put together, reminding me of Brad Pitt. "And I'm Agent Morris with the FBI." He gave me his card.

Detective Brook pulled some papers out and spoke. "Okay, April, when was the last time that you talked to your uncle?"

Figuring that they already had that info, I told them. "I was on the phone with him the night that everything happened."

"In fact, you were on the phone when everything was happening, am I right? From his phone records and when 911 calls started coming in, you and he were talking at that moment."

"I know that now."

"So, you're saying that you didn't hear any gunshots while y'all were talking?"

"No, I heard a lot of them. They had to be shooting for at least a few minutes."

"And what did you do after hearing this?" He wrote something down before he asked me his next question.

"I hung the phone up. I didn't want to hear that."

"So, you heard your uncle being murdered, but you didn't call the police?"

"I really thought it was him doing the shooting. He told me to hold up, then it sounded like a war going on, so I hung up. I knew he has been having problems, so I didn't want to throw him off his square."

Detective Lowe jumped in. "What do you know about those incidents?"

"Nothing more than people came around his house and started shooting a few times. Uncle Cash don't talk to me about that kind of stuff."

"But you know the things he does? You know enough about his drug dealing and gang activities to know it's a good chance that it could have been him shooting. Or him getting shot at isn't nothing out of the normal," the detective asked.

"Yeah, which is why I have very little dealings with him. I don't know enough, and I don't want my family to get caught up in that kind of stuff. I lost my parents to the streets, and now I lost my uncle. I'd rather not lose nobody else to that dumb shit." My phone started ringing. I looked at them to answer it, and when Detective Lowe nodded his head, I answered and put it on speaker.

"Hello."

"April, this is Kenny McGill. I was contacted by friends of your family, and they say that you may need an attorney."

"No, I was just asked to come in and answer a few questions and see if maybe I can help them find my uncle's killer."

"Well, wait till I get there before you talk to them."

Before I could say anything, Detective Brook said, "Hello, Mr. McGill. This is Detective Brook with Chicago PD, and I can assure you that Mrs. Thompson is not under any suspicion. She's here as a witness only."

"Did you read her rights to her?"

"I know that you're used to dealing with criminals, Mr. McGill, but this isn't one of them. She is a witness and nothing more, so there is no reason to advise her of criminal rights."

"Okay, but I'll like to stay on the phone with her just in case."

"That's fine. We're about to wrap this up anyways."

Detective Lowe started asking me more questions. "Okay, so besides hearing gunshots, did you hear anything? Maybe somebody else talking or a noise?"

"It wasn't clear, but it sounded like they were talking in Spanish or something like that."

They looked at each other, and Agent Morris spoke for the first time. "You have been in contact with your parents a lot lately. Are they mad enough to have had Cash killed?"

"Hell naw. My daddy would give his life for his brother, and the only person my mom will go against my daddy for is me, so ain't no way they had nothing to do with this." I didn't think they would go this way, but I knew that they had nothing to go off of.

"Well, I'd think that would change if they were able to find out that he wore a wire on them and is the only reason that we had a case."

"That's not true. My uncle may have been many things, but a snitch wasn't one of them," I spoke up. I couldn't believe I was defending

Cash, but I believed what I said. There were too many fucked up things people could say about Cash without lying. So, that was what they needed to stick with. Their lies wouldn't fly with me, even if I did hate him.

Agent Morris pulled papers out of his folder and passed them to me. I started flipping through them, reading a little on each page. It showed from the time he started working with them til after he got out. Some of the things that were talked about were things that I knew for sure only him, Daddy, or Moms knew because I was around when it was talked about.

"And if that's not enough, this should be," Agent Morris said as he pulled a small recording device out and pressed play. Cash's voice was telling the same shit that I was reading.

I hated Cash enough to have him killed, so I didn't know how I could hate him any more than that, but he betrayed us in a way that I didn't think anybody would've seen.

I didn't realize I was crying until Agent Morris handed me some tissue, and the next thing he said was like a knife in my back.

"If your parents weren't involved, which just might be the case since there are only a few that know about these files and the name that goes with it, we believe that his new connect was involved. Cash contacted us saying that he would give them up if we put him in witness protection. He was really scared." He slid me more papers and spoke. "We were working on setting everything up, and we believe that the connect got wind of it."

I was raised to be tough and not show my emotions, but that fast, I saw in my head the Feds fucking up my life for a second time. Even though I never approved of it, Bishop called himself doing the right thing, and Cash still would've gotten down on him.

I was stuck. I couldn't say anything, just wanted to get out of there. Thankfully, Detective Brook realized the interview was over.

"April, we know this is a lot to take in, and you're hurt by this news, but if you hear anything, we need to know. These kind of people sometimes go after family members too. It would be best if we can catch them now. Feel free to call any of us, no matter what it is."

I could only nod. I didn't trust myself to say anything, so I grabbed my phone and got up.

"Go home to your family, April. You have no control over who your family is but keep doing what you can not to become like them," Detective Brook said as he led me out.

As I walked out, I thought about all the people I was mad at. Bishop because he allowed this nigga to come close to our family and almost take us down.

My daddy because he was the smartest man I knew, and the only way he didn't see it was because he didn't want to.

But I was mad at myself more than anything since if I wouldn't have made an issue about it, Cash would have never known anything, and if I had asked for help before Corn figured out what I was on, then Cash would have been out the way.

When I got back in the car, I told Bishop everything that they told me. He listened, and when I got to the part about Cash setting it up to tell on us, I knew he had some of the same thoughts I did.

I was going to tell him about Juan and how he was trying to kill Cash for me, but I didn't because I didn't want to mention Corn, but I was right either way. For now, I just felt like going home and spending time with my family because the thought of me losing them had me scared and wondering if all the money and power was worth it.

CHAPTER NINETEEN

Bishop

After everything went down, I had to get an outside view. I hit Hectic up to see when he'd be in the city again. He was busy on some important business, but since he heard about everything that went on, he allowed something that we'd never done. We talked business over the phone.

I told him everything from why we made the choice to have Cash killed to what April told me about him about to get down on us with the Feds.

"Hustler, think about the situation with Lil Tone. Your intention was good with him, and you wanted for him the same shit that you wanted for yourself because that was your brother. But he was still able to do all the things that he did to hurt your family. So, tell me why you would be surprised that somebody would do what Cash was trying to do?"

It made sense now, but that wasn't how I was seeing it then, so I told him why I did it.

"I don't know. It's like his brother wanted him to have some kind of role, and given it's April's blood, I wanted to give him a chance." Even though I said it, it sounded really stupid coming out of my mouth.

"Damn, hustler, for you to be so damn smart, you do some dumb shit sometimes. In so many words, you just let somebody else move a piece on your chess board. Why would you allow a person that has nothing to lose dictate your movement?"

I thought about it, and he was right. I had to stop giving a fuck about everybody else's wants when it didn't benefit my family.

"Yeah, you're right. I fucked up."

"But with no consequences that we can see. Thankfully, we were able to learn from this shit. The question now is how are you going to deal with April's dad? He still has pull in the streets, so he might feel some kind of way about this shit."

"I'm not worried about that. We're going to see him this weekend, and I guess we'll see how it goes. The lawyer said that since Cash is dead that we can get those statements, and since he didn't know about that, I'm sure he'll see it the same way any street nigga would. Either way, it's whatever."

"I know this never had to come up, but you're a big piece in our operation, and you got a lot of people on your side. We have connections, and if you ever need help, just let me know. It doesn't matter if it's on the streets or in the joint."

As we ended the call, I could only put my head down. There was so many things going on, and I just felt like yelling. My mind was trying to think ahead, but I kept thinking about how Cash tried to give us up while they claimed not to have shit. What if they were just trying to see what we knew and were watching us?

Despite Hectic thinking Dolla could have a problem, I still thought that he would be on April's side, no matter what. But if they wanted to take it there, we had enough shooters where we could take them niggas on. Yeah, we didn't know who was on their side, but we had not only our people, but there were still so many that didn't fuck with Cash and his guys just off the way they were getting down on them before we took over. We could get them to ride with us too.

"Bishop, what if he doesn't understand?" April asked. She hadn't said anything about what we were going to see her dad for the entire ride there but said that as soon as we pulled into the parking lot.

"What's there not to understand if we just tell him what it is? Not only did the nigga go back on his word, he stole from us. If that's not enough, he was the one that told on them, and he was planning on telling on us. No matter how you look at it, Cash had to go, and I'm not going to lose not a second of sleep for having it done. If he can't understand that, then him being your dad or not, we don't need to be dealing with him."

"I just know that he sees no wrong in Cash, so he'll try to flip that shit. That's what he did to my mommy."

"Let's just get this shit done. We need to only worry about ourselves sometimes because it's clear we won't be able to please everybody."

And that's what I was going to be doing going forward. After thinking about everything I talked to Hectic about, I realized that even with niggas that fucked with each other, somebody had their own missions that only benefitted them.

Ever since I got locked up, I was hesitant about going to any jail or prison, and April had to think I was nervous for the wrong reasons because she grabbed my hand.

"Baby, we in this together. Nothing he says will change anything. So, stop stressing about this shit."

I gave her a little laugh. I didn't feel the need to correct her because a part of me thought she was speaking to herself.

We got to our table and waited so long that I was going to ask the guard what was taking so long. Then I saw Dolla walking toward us, and I could tell that this wasn't going to go as smooth as I hoped.

April stood up to give him a hug, but he just sat down and got right down to business.

"Y'all better be here to tell me that y'all found out who killed my brother and that at least the main one is dead and the rest will follow soon," Dolla spoke.

He was looking between us, but I was paying attention to April, who was still just standing there. I could tell that she was hurt, but she came and sat down.

"Hello to you too, Daddy. It's nice to see you too."

"I don't got time for all that bullshit. Tell me y'all at least know who did it or working on finding out. Somebody fuckin' answer me! I'm not talkin' to myself!" Dolla yelled when neither of us answered him.

"Naw, Daddy. We haven't even been trying to find out who did it. To us, it'll be like looking for a ghost because your brother did so many niggas in the streets wrong that it really could've been anybody."

"April, the fuckin' streets talk. So, what have you been hearing?" Dolla asked.

"That somebody he trusted had to set him up because he was scared of niggas shooting at him every time he popped his head out these last few months."

"He wasn't scared of shit. If he was set up like they said, then who did he trust like that? The list can't be that long."

April got quiet again and put her head down. When she picked her head back up and looked at me, she had tears in her eyes, and I knew what she was about to say even before she started talking.

"Daddy, I know you're not going to like it, but I refuse to try to hide what I've done, especially when I did the right thing in the situation."

"What the fuck are you trying to say, April?" Dolla asked in a low tone. I could tell he already knew but wanted to hear the words from her own mouth.

"Your brother was a snake, and he didn't give a fuck about nobody but himself. Not you, me, or anybody else and I wasn't about to let him take us down. I had him killed."

I focused on Dolla, and I knew if it was anybody else telling him this, he would've been trying to kill them. But as they say... if looks could kill.

"April, you came here to tell me you had my brother, your own fuckin' uncle, killed? I don't think that it's many acceptable reasons that you can tell me but please tell me why you would do something like that without coming to ask me first."

"Daddy, I don't answer to no one, and if I feel something has to be done, then I take care of it as I see fit. I live behind my decisions, but the best reason that I can give you is to protect my family," April spoke, standing her ground.

"But what the fuck did he do that made you feel that you had to protect your so-called family because you're forgetting that he was your family too."

"I found this out after the fact, but not only did he wear a wire on you and my mom, which is the reason that I don't have my parents out there to help me in hard times, but he was trying to set it up to wear a wire on me and my husband, which would have left my babies in the same position. I just refuse to accept that."

When Dolla didn't say anything, April continued to speak. "I didn't have to be taught not to snitch. When the people got y'all and tried to get me to talk, I didn't. He should have known better too."

She finally looked at him. "Daddy, if it was Bishop telling on somebody, I would do the same thing to him."

I felt I had to say something because I had given Dolla my word that I would do what I could for his brother, but if his brother crossed me that I'd do him like any other nigga in the streets.

"On some real shit, you know the streets. You ran them, and it's like I'm following your blueprint because April and Corn taught me a lot of what I know. They learned from you and Top Hat. So, you know if a nigga played with your money, you going to do the same shit. Before you get to talking about how money ain't shit, the biggest thing is respect, and his actions were disrespectful. I'm not accepting that."

"But you want me to accept you killing my brother? And at the end of the day, over some petty money?"

"Dolla, I don't know where you're trying to take this, but you're my wife's dad. I know how much she loves you, so I'm just going to keep my words to myself."

"Don't hold back. You're man enough to call hits, so be man enough to speak your fuckin' mind."

I didn't want to take it there with him, not wanting to put April in a fucked-up position, but I wasn't accepting any nigga calling me out.

"Dolla, you not a stupid nigga. I did what I did for my reasons, but if I would've waited any longer, dude would've fucked up my family. That's something that I won't accept, and it's on you to accept or not accept what you want. He was your brother."

April tried to grab Dolla's hand, but he pulled it back. "Daddy, we were treating him better than he deserved, and he was going to take me from my kids. I learned about that when they told me he wore a wire on y'all, and you sitting here trying to get into it with the one man that would move the world for me."

"April, I don't care about what he did, but since you want to go against family then consider me dead just like my brother. I'm not going to be involved in nothing you got going on, so don't come to me for nothing else."

I expected April to start crying since I knew how she felt about her dad, but she didn't. "Daddy, it's clear that you only see one person as your family, but mine is bigger than that. Anybody that goes against our best interest will get the same thing Cash got. Once you sit back and realize that you're wrong, don't let your pride get in the way and get at me."

Dolla just shook his head. "Don't wait up for that call. I know your mom is going to take your side. So, tell her not to bring that shit my way." He got up and walked away without looking back.

I grabbed April's hand. "Let's go. If that's how he feels, then let it be."

She waited till we got back in the car before she said, "You know he didn't even seem surprised when I said that Cash wore a wire on them. I think that he knew the whole time. I will always love my daddy, but I swear that I just lost all respect for him."

"As long as you're not doubting what we had to do, then we can keep it moving. We did what we had to, and by doing it, we still got our family and freedom. If anybody wants to question that, then their values are all the way fucked up, and they can't be trusted," I told April.

"That was something to learn from, but it's behind us, so let's get back to us."

The only problem was that it wasn't behind us. We were going to have to show niggas just what we were about.

CHAPTER TWENTY

April

OF ALL MY GIRLS, I ONLY HAD TIME TO BE AROUND BABY D AND Mona but never to hang out and kick it like we wanted to. It was always business, but now, I was ready to have some fun.

"Girl, why didn't you tell me we were going bowling? I would've worn some come get me shorts, so these niggas could see me when I roll the ball," Baby D said when she saw me pull up to the bowling alley.

"What the shorts that only got the waistline part?" I joked about the kind of shorts she always wore that barely covered anything.

"What? Are you trying to fuck with an old white man and give him a heart attack? Ain't no nigga that we trying to fuck with going to be up in here," Mona said as we got out the backseat of the car.

"First off, April, if it was a problem, then a business wouldn't let me in. They cover enough to be legal, so they're good enough for me, and Mona, yo ass sleep. All the niggas with the bag be at the bowling alley. I don't got to tell you though. You about to see for yourself."

"Let me find out y'all been bowling alley hoeing," Mona said to us and started laughing.

"Shit, April's a married ho. She can't do shit like that, but I always bump into Twin and 'em in this bitch. You the only one that don't know what's going on."

We walked in, and the niggas seemed to be in there deeper than normal. We went up to pay for a lane.

"We're booked right now, but if you're willing to wait, we'll give you ten dollars off and a free drink for each of you at the bar," the lady behind the desk said.

"Yeah, that's fine. We want three games for four people." I ordered our games and paid for them.

As we walked away, Mona said, "April, it's only three of us. Who you got coming?"

"Nobody, she already here. My girl is never far from me. You just don't see her." When I said it, they knew that I was talking about Miracle.

"That's some scary shit," Mona said.

"Bitch, that's the point. You want somebody that's nice protecting you? What I want to know is why you're the only one with a bodyguard? I want one of them sexy, crazy niggas watching me all day. I'll make sure to give him a tip every night," Baby D spoke.

I laughed at her ass. "Y'all dumb as hell."

We went to the bar and got ourselves some drinks. I knew niggas were going to flock to us as soon as we sat down. I knew that was what my girls wanted, so I let them do them and stayed in the cut.

"Damn, Ma, you don't know how to talk, or you feel you too good for a nigga?" There were six niggas around us trying to talk some weak ass game. One of them focused on me, but I turned, letting him know that I wasn't interested.

He started to say something, but Mona cut him off. "She ain't here for that, but I'm nasty enough to take two of y'all."

"See, them the kind of bitches I hate. Come out then don't want to give a nigga no play till I flash some money."

"Call yo mama a bitch and leave my girl alone." I liked that Mona was doing the talking because she was going to match whatever he had to say and didn't give a fuck.

"Fuck all that. I'll give you a hundred just to lick my dick." He pulled out a small roll of money. "Or what, you a freak like your girl? I'll give you a band to take on the whole team." He started counting off bills. "What's your price?"

I finally had to say something. "Look, it's enough females here to pick from, so find something safe to do before shit go bad for you."

"Okay, she can talk. You like it rough? I can get with that if that's what you're into."

I looked at one of his homies. "Your homie must be drunk. Can you take him somewhere else, so his words don't get him in trouble?"

"Yeah, foe, you tweaking. Shorty bad, but we chasing pussy, not looking for a wife," he told the dude that was in my face.

"You right, but mark my words, this bitch going to be all over my dick when we take these streets over. On the foe, I'm going to make her suck my dog's dick." He walked off laughing.

I let his disrespect slide, but I thought about him thinking that he — or anybody else — was going to take the streets from us.

Baby D came up, rubbing my back. "Girl, don't pay that nigga no mind. He a fuckin' bum. We can go somewhere else if you want."

"You got me fucked up. I'm about to beat y'all ass in some bowling. Me and Miracle against y'all two. Don't try to get out of it now." We sat there and talked shit for thirty minutes before they called our name.

Just as we were walking toward the lane, Mona said, "Hell naw, girl, that's Bishop right there. And he walking toward that boy like he 'bout to kill something." She pointed to where he was, and I knew they were on bullshit. It was Bishop, Bull, and at least ten more of the guys.

Just when I started walking toward them, Miracle was on my side. "I had to make that call. When he walked away, he said that he was going to wait for you to come out and slap you. If it was just him, we could have taken care of it, but they ass too deep."

I nodded, knowing she did right. I just wanted to stop Bishop from doing something crazy. I still had my heels on and was walking as fast as I could, but there was no way that I was going to be able to stop them from doing whatever they had planned.

I got close enough to hear Bishop say, "So, you want to slap my wife?" He didn't even give him a chance to say shit before he slapped the shit out of him.

Some of his guys tried to move, but Bull said, "You do, and this bitch is going up."

Bishop had already punched him twice and put him on the floor. He would have kept going if I wouldn't have stopped him.

"Bishop, stop!" I yelled. He didn't look back at me, but he stepped back and let the dude get back up before he slapped him again so hard that he fell.

"Next time you better know who the fuck you're talking to. You lucky my homie talked me out of shooting you in your mouth, bitch ass nigga."

One of his guys, who I now realized I recognized from Cash's block, raised both of his hands.

"I'm not on that. He didn't know shorty was April. Blame that shit on the drugs. Foe a good nigga." He looked at me. "Sorry 'bout ya uncle but now that he's gone, I'm taking over. At a better time, do you think we can sit down and talk some business over?"

"What they call you?" I asked him.

"Mello."

"Mello, I'm April. Now, what business do you want to talk about?"

"You want to talk about it right here?" he asked.

"My bowling game got messed up, so I might as well make some money. What better time than now? Plus, the streets don't stand still for nobody." I sat down at the table and waited on him to sit with me.

"Look, I know that you're against charging for the blocks like we used to do, so you been hitting Cash with fifteen keys every month. I just want to make sure that nothing changed."

"Look, Mello… Cash didn't make that happen. I did. So, why would anything change now that he's gone?"

BISHOP

I just stood back and listened to this Mello nigga try to play April, but she saw where he was going, so I didn't say shit.

"That's good to hear. So, when do you think we can get the first shipment, and how are we going to do this?" Mello asked.

"Whenever you're ready, just get up with us, and we can make it happen," April said.

I had to shut this down. I didn't want this nigga to get shit twisted any further than he already did.

"Hold up. I'm…" April held up her hand, and I stopped talking to hear her out.

"If you can handle our new prices, then you can get as many as you want."

"But that's not what I'm talking about. Since I'm taking over…"

I cut him off now. "She knows what you were talking about. That shit died with Cash; he was lucky to be getting it, so ain't no next up shit going on. Now she said that if you can pay for it, she'll do business with you. So, can you pay the price, or are we wasting our time? Because real shit, I was in the middle of something and need to get back to it."

"If we ain't gettin' the fifteen keys, then we gon' get back to collecting dues from all the blocks we own. We'll find somebody else to cop from since I see y'all bad for business."

I walked a little closer to this Mello nigga, so he could hear me clear over the music, and I didn't have to yell. "Mello, let's get this clear. If you — or any of your people — go touch a dollar off any block, then you're going to get more than you're looking for."

Mello clapped three times and leaned closer to me. "Bishop, ain't nobody scared of this show you putting on. You can save all that shit."

Bull tried to get between us, but I stopped him. He still said what he wanted. "Nigga, you need to watch who you're talking to because you better believe this ain't no show." Bull stepped back at my side. "Bishop, just give me the word and I'm going to put this nigga thoughts all over the place."

"Naw, we gon' let him fuck up first. Then, I'll let him see if this a show. He won't see the end of it."

Mello stood. "Well, I guess I'll see you in the streets because threats don't move me. Don't pay up by the end of the month and watch how I come for them dues or shut them blocks down." He walked away, and all his guys followed.

"You should let me handle this shit before it starts. He told you that he'll do the shit, and to me, that's just as good as doing it. We can catch their whole team right down the street. Just give me the go."

"Yeah, he might be stupid enough to do it, but let him think about it. If he drives down on one block, we'll take care of it," I informed him.

I could tell Bull was mad; he shook his head. "My nigga, you got it, but after this, I'm not asking no more. If I see a problem, I'm taking care of it. That's my word."

"You do that then. I'm ready to change shit up anyways. So, let's see how this plays out. If the streets need to see what we can get on besides getting money, then that's what it is." I knew I had to keep control over everything and everybody around me, but I also understood that at some point, I just had to let things go the way they had to and let people do what they were there to do.

EPILOGUE

Bishop

I was so busy with moving shit for Jesus and José that I lost track of the days, and it wasn't till I got back to back calls from an unknown number that I realized it was about time for distribution.

I answered the second call. "Who is this?"

"This Mello. I just wanted to know if you reconsidered and want to keep shit how it is."

"Who gave you my number?" I asked, confused.

"I know people. But that should be the least of your worries. I know y'all young niggas like to make moves off pride, but if you think about it, why should we start a war when shit is sweet in the streets right now?"

"And it's still going to be sweet for me. My wife told you what it was. If my pride got in the way, then I'll be saying that shit is dead, but I'm not your average nigga. That said, come with the money and you can go about your business and get money like everybody else."

"You made a deal to keep the blocks open, and that's how it's gone stay, or we're going to go back to the old ways."

"I'm not about to keep talking in circles, but you must got some bogus info because of that fifteen. He was paying for five. Five were his brother's, who don't want it no more, and Cash was getting five because he was my wife's uncle. Nothing had to do with the blocks. That's our shit to control, and that's not about to change for nothing. So, do what you see fit, and we'll handle it when the time comes." I hung up, not giving the conversation a second thought. When the first of the month came and went, I waited on his call to talk business, but it was two weeks before he made his choice.

Bull came into the house and found me in the front room going over some spreadsheets Kayla wanted me to look over. I could tell something was wrong by the look on his face. Sitting the papers on the table, I gave Bull my full attention.

"Bishop, I just got a call, and them niggas is on the move. They just drove down Gladys deep as hell. I told my people to stand down, but one of the workers started shootin'. They shot back and hit him in the leg, but he was all good," Bull informed.

"Okay, let's go then." This nigga made his move, and I wanted to make sure he didn't enjoy a minute of it.

"Slow down. Right now, they just riding through, making threats. I think he just wants to get your attention, so he can try to make a deal. If he wanted trouble, then he'll be coming a whole different way. You know where I stand, but it's on you how you want to play it out."

"He got my attention if that's what he wanted, but I'm not trying to talk. I told him already if he makes a move, then he going to see what I'm going to do."

"So, we about to clear all the workers off the blocks. I got my boy following them. I know it would be too much to ask you to sit back. So, get your vest on and your guns cocked. This ain't no movie shit. I'm not trying to have you in the middle of the street having a shootout."

"Just take me there. Shooting ain't my thing unless I need to, but the new me gon' let these niggas know I'll come out with my team. Hectic probably won't like it, but I think it's going to take that for me to get real respect from the streets."

"That makes my job easier. Once you give us the go, I'm going to get you in the car before we fuck them niggas up, and you better believe the streets will know."

"And then my takeover will be official." I cocked my gun back before walking out the house, ready for war.

To Be Continued...

Despite The Odds 3
Coming Soon!!

OTHER BOOKS BY

Urban Aint Dead

Tales 4rm Da Dale

The Hottest Summer Ever

Hittin' Licks For The Holidays: Atlanta

Wet Dreams On Lockdown: The Nurse

How To Publish A Book From Prison

How To Invest In The Stock Market From Prison

By **Elijah R. Freeman**

Despite The Odds

By **Juhnell Morgan**

Good Girls Gone Rogue

Good Girls Gone Rogue 2

By **Manny Black**

Hittaz

Hittaz 2

Hittaz 3

Hittaz 4

Hittaz 5

Hittaz 6

Coldhearted

Coldhearted 2

Coldhearted 3

By **Lou Garden Price, Sr.**

Charge It To The Game

Charge It To The Game 2

Charge It To The Game 3

A Summer To Remember With My Hitta

Snatched Up By A Hitta

Santa Sent Me A Real One For Christmas

Wet Dreams On Lockdown: The Unit Manager

Thug Me The Right Way 2

Thug Me The Right Way 3

Seizing A Gangsta's Heart For The Summer

Yours For The Taking

Wrapped Up In A Hitta's Love For Christmas

By **Nai**

A Set Up For Revenge

A Set Up For Revenge 2

Wet Dreams On Lockdown: The Librarian

By **Ashley Williams**

Trickin' On A Heaux For Christmas

Homie Hoppin' For The Holidays

Wet Dreams On Lockdown: The Female C.O

Letters Of His Love

By **Telia Teanna**

The State's Witness

The State's Witness 2

The State's Witness 3

This Time Won't You Save Me

This Time Won't You Save Me 2

His Summer Side Piece

A Holiday Heist

Healing The Heart Of A Detroit Gangsta

By **Kyiris Ashley**

Stuck In The Trenches

Stuck In The Trenches 2

By **Huff Tha Great**

Melted The Heart Of A Menace

Wet Dreams On Lockdown: Lieutenant Grace

By **P. Wise**

Merry Trapmas

By **Mia Sky**

Thug Me The Right Way

By **DiamondATL & Nai**

Wet Dreams On Lockdown: The Counselor

By **Paris Iman**

Wet Dreams On Lockdown: The Male C.O

By **Tamyra Griffin**

Wet Dreams On Lockdown: The Captain

By **TN Jones**

Wet Dreams On Lockdown: The Warden

By **Shawnice**

Atlantastan

Atlantastan 2

By **Chris Green**

IN The Streetz

IN The Streetz 2

IN The Streetz 3

IN The Streetz 4

By **Tron Hill**

Hittin' Licks For The Holidays: New York

By **Freshh Moneyy**

Coming Soon From
URBAN AINT DEAD

The Hottest Summer Ever 2
THE G-CODE
Tales 4rm Da Dale 2
How To Build Your Credit From Prison
By **Elijah R. Freeman**

Good Girls Gone Rogue 3
By **Manny Black**

Despite The Odds 3
By **Juhnell Morgan**

Foreva Your Gangsta
By **Nai**

This Time Won't You Save Me 3
By **Kyiris Ashley**

Atlantastan 3
By **Chris Green**

IN The Streetz 5
By **Tron Hill**

Bandemic
By Freshh Moneyy

BOOKS BY

URBAN AINT DEAD's C.E.O

<u>Elijah R. Freeman</u>

Triggadale 1, 2 & 3

Tales 4rm Da Dale

The Hottest Summer Ever

Murda Was The Case 1, 2 & 3

Hittin' Licks For The Holidays: Atlanta

Wet Dreams On Lockdown: The Nurse

How To Publish A Book From Prison

How To Invest In The Stock Market From Prison

STAY CONNECTED

Follow
Elijah R. Freeman
On Social Media
FB: Elijah R. Freeman
IG: @the_future_of_urban_fiction